Love Entwined

M.C. DECKER

Dedication

To my Nachos—Gia Riley and Mandi Beck—I'd be lost in this world without you. We started out as strangers and soon became friends. You've become the sisters I never knew I wanted, but soon realized I couldn't live without. Here's to: #BitchesNachos #Shenanigans #BreathinEasy #timezones #whistles #P4D #BigGulp

Prologue

JAMES BENTLEY

ONE FINAL TIME, I patted my side pocket making sure the ring box was securely planted in its rightful place, before getting behind the wheel of the Corvette convertible I'd rented for the evening. I wanted the night to be perfect. I'd never had the opportunity to take Ireland to prom when we were in high school and when she told me that she'd never gone at all, I knew immediately that I wanted to do something special for her. Call me pussy-whipped, but at least I knew I'd be buried deep inside hers later tonight. This senior—more like senior citizen, I thought to myself—would definitely be scoring this evening.

I was sure Katie had already shown Ireland the gown I'd purchased for her to wear. I'd also scheduled an afternoon appointment of pampering for both of them at a local spa. I really had no idea what girls did for hours in those places, but Katie said she would handle it. You could call me a complete idiot for handing my credit card over to that woman, but nothing would be too extravagant for my Shamrock.

Needing to make a quick stop at the architectural firm to pick up some blueprints, I then went on to the construction site to check the progress of my most recent design project. I didn't want any interruptions or surprises tonight—just Ireland's toned legs entwined with mine in bed, or maybe wrapped around my waist as I slammed into her, pressed up against the wall.

I had about thirty minutes to spare before the limousine I'd rented for Ireland was scheduled to drop her off at Iridescence. Located on the sixteenth floor of the MotorCity Casino Hotel, Iridescence was known as the hidden gem of Detroit and I'd been able to secure the entire restaurant for just the two of us.

We'd been there once before and Ireland had raved about the floor-to-ceiling windows which overlooked the city with a view of the Ambassador Bridge. Every time we'd driven past the building since then, she commented about how much she wanted to dine there again. I told her we could go anytime, but she always insisted it was too expensive and we always wound up taking a five-dollar carryout pizza home from the local pizza parlor.

I'm not sure she would ever get used to the fact that I was part owner in a very successful firm and had more than enough money to drop on a nice dinner. But, tonight and every night from now on, I wanted her to know that everything I had was hers—including my heart, and my future. Tonight, I was going to ask her to be a part of that future as my wife.

I was surprised to see my business partner/best friend's car in the parking lot when I pulled up to the construction site. No doubt he was going to bust my balls for my choice of wardrobe tonight.

"Hey Greg, I didn't expect to see you here. After all, it's after four in the afternoon and a Saturday no less," I quipped, grabbing a hard hat before stepping onto the site.

"Fuck you, asshole," he retorted without looking up from the design he was poring over. "And, I really should be asking you the same thing. Katie told me you had some top secret date planned for you and Ireland tonight.

"I take it she was right since you're dressed in that god-awful penguin suit," he joked, momentarily taking his eyes off the blueprints he'd been studying.

"Yeah, tonight's the night," I told him, patting my side pocket once again. "I just wanted to make a quick stop here to make sure everything was in order and then I'm taking Ireland to our prom at Iridescence. Didn't Katie tell you all about it?"

"Yeah, she did, but I honestly tuned her out after she spoke the first few words. I love my wife, really I do, but you know how she can go on and on," he said.

"And on," I laughed.

"Right. So, I flipped on an episode of *Sons of Anarchy* and nodded my head a few times. She isn't any the wiser. But, congrats man. I'm happy for the two of you even if you are lame as fuck with setting up this whole prom thing."

"Yeah, yeah. I knew you were gonna give me shit for it. Honestly, I didn't give Staci the proposal that she deserved and maybe that's one of many reasons our marriage was a joke. I was a senior in college who'd just knocked up his girlfriend and thought I needed to get down on one knee to be a real man. I didn't do either of us any favors. Had I known she was going to fuck other guys the entire time we were married I would have fought for custody of Tanner and hit the road."

"Sorry I even mentioned it, man. Go to your prom and put a ring on the girl of your dreams. You know Ireland is like the little sister I never had and I know you'll treat her right."

"Thanks, Greg. I wasn't really looking for your approval, but since Ireland doesn't have any family, I guess it really does mean a lot," I said, patting him on the shoulder.

"Now I only have twenty minutes before I'm meeting Ireland and I need to check out the archway and make sure it's up to our client's standards. Clark wasn't pleased with the results when he stopped by day before yesterday and I told him I would take care of it by Monday. You know how fucking picky that man can be," I yelled down as I began climbing the scaffolding.

Clark and Kelly Miller were known as some of the snobbiest restauranteurs in metro Detroit. Clark, especially, walked around like he had a constant pole stuck up his ass and everything had to be perfect down to the exact dimensions of the floor tiling. However, he'd believed in me since I began working in the field over a decade ago and I'd since designed every one of his restaurants in the state. I wasn't about to let him down now, especially over a fucking archway.

"You might want to grab a few of the safety hooks before you get up there too high. The workers were complaining about some of the planks slipping earlier today," Greg called out.

"Nah, I'll be fine. I'll just be up there a minute and I don't really want to get any wrinkles on this—what did you call it—penguin suit. Besides, I have a thick skull and this hard hat will protect me," I said, tapping on the thick, yellow plastic.

"I'm surprised you were willing to put on the hat—wouldn't want it to ruin your hair," Greg yelled back.

"Safety first, fucker," I shouted, just as my feet began to slip from under me. I reached for the guardrail, but only grabbed a fistful of air as I began my descent down to the cold, unforgiving concrete. I barely heard Greg's muffled scream through my own rapidly beating heart. And then there was only silence.

Three Days Later

EVERYTHING WAS FUZZY as I began hearing voices off in the distance.

"Jamie—Jamie, open your eyes for us again? Come back to us."

I opened my eyes and was greeted by my favorite pair of blues. So many emotions rested inside Staci's eyes. Why did she look so forlorn, so confused even? I looked over her shoulder and saw Tanner, our son, standing behind her. For some reason, he looked taller, older even.

"It's OK, I've come back to you—to both of you. I'm here

now," I whispered, my throat still raw from the ventilator tube.

I wasn't sure what had happened, but I knew I was in a hospital room. I'd heard doctors and nurses discuss my accident, but I wasn't sure of the details or the severity of my injuries. I remember waking up and calling for her earlier, but instead I was greeted by a stranger in my room. There was something about her—something comforting and so familiar even. I assumed she was just a nurse and probably made all of her patients feel that way. She held my hand and I swear she even had tears in her eyes, but I could have been imagining it, or just so hopped up on pain medication that my mind was playing tricks on me. After all, why would a nurse cry for me?

"Oh thank God you're awake," Staci said with relief. "I'll go get the doctor. He should probably examine you now that you're awake."

"Just give me a minute with you," I pleaded. "I just want to hold you."

My entire body was screaming in pain, but in that moment I didn't care that my arm was bandaged and in a sling, or that every time I took a breath my chest burned. I would worry about the doctors later. All I wanted and cared about right now was my wife and my son.

"Jamie," she said, pulling back. "Do you remember anything—anything about the accident—about falling?"

"No, I didn't even know I'd fallen. It's all pretty fuzzy. I only remember waking up briefly and calling out for you. The nurse said she would get you."

"The nurse?" she questioned.

It was when Staci turned her head that I noticed the woman, who I assumed had been my nurse, sitting on the bench positioned near the window. She did in fact have tears streaming down her face, but I still had no idea who she was or why she was crying.

"Jamie, she isn't your nurse. That's Ireland," my wife

explained.

"Ireland?" I knew an Ireland once, but we hadn't seen each other in nearly two decades. Why would Ireland be in my hospital room?

"I don't understand. Why is Ireland here?"

"Because you were planning on marrying her, Jamie."

"Staci, you aren't making any sense. How can I marry another woman when you're my wife?"

"Jamie, we haven't been married for nearly a year," she said, biting down on her lip. "I really think I should go get the doctor now."

Her words stunned me. My world as I knew it was crashing around me. I wanted nothing more than for deep sleep to consume me once again. I shut my eyes and prayed that when I opened them this nightmare would be over and I would remember—everything.

Chapter One

IRELAND

Six months earlier

I FINGERED THE silver, heart-shaped locket around my neck as I waited for my best friend to step out of her bridal suite. I always envisioned this day when I was growing up, but in my dreams I was always the little girl in the puffy, white dress and flowing veil and not the one wearing a strapless, Merlot bridesmaid dress playing second fiddle to the bride.

I was a bit of a tomboy as a child, not really into dresses—truth be told, I still preferred a silk pantsuit to this chiffon number that Katie insisted worked perfectly with my sun-kissed skin tone. But, on those rare occasions when I could convince my then best friend, Bentley, to dress up and play pretend wedding with me, I transformed into a girly princess.

My mom had even bought me a fluffy white dress and draping veil for such occasions. Bentley always wore jeans and a white, button-down shirt with a matching denim vest. I always tried to get him to wear a white suit as he had the day we'd met, but he always pouted and stomped off at even a mention of the idea. I chuckled to myself at the memory. "I miss you," I whispered to myself, opening the locket to thumb over the pictures

I'd placed in it.

My dreams turned into nightmares the day they all left me. From that moment on, I vowed not to let anyone in again—that was until Katie's family moved to Knoxville and she started at my high school. I'd been forced to move into a group home for children across the state when my mom died. I hated calling it an orphanage, but that's what it was and who I was—*an orphan*. The word seemed to have such a stigma about it. When most people found out I was an orphan they would always look at me in one of two ways.

They would either give me a look of pity, or one of mistrust. I guess being an orphan meant I was a bad kid, destined to live a life of crime on the streets. When in reality, my only wrongdoing was not having any parents. It was not a crime that my family had died, but in strangers' eyes, I'd already been convicted.

Katie was different. She looked at me like a regular kid—like a teenage girl who had a family. She only lived in Knoxville for about five months, but in those months she made me forget the pain and loneliness I'd been feeling. She also made me forget—*him*. It took nearly two years, but someone had finally eased the pain of losing everyone I'd ever loved.

I remember crying for days at the thought of her leaving me like everyone else had. Her family's newly built home was nearing completion in another school district about thirty miles away and I knew the time we had together was limited. She would be moving and I would be alone—again. One by one everyone I'd ever loved had left me.

"You're leaving tomorrow, aren't you?" I sobbed. *"I'm going to be all alone again."*

"I am leaving tomorrow, Ireland, but my parents and I have a surprise for you. I couldn't say anything sooner because they had to go through the court first, but you're coming with me," Katie exclaimed, *jumping up and down.*

"What do you mean I'm going with you? Like for a vacation?" I

asked.

"No, you're going to come and live with us in our new house. We're going to be sisters."

I couldn't believe the words I was hearing.

"What? How?" I questioned, scratching my head.

"My parents went to your social worker and got everything approved with the courts. They could adopt you if you'd like—to make it official—but since we'll be eighteen next year anyways, your social worker said that adoption wouldn't be necessary for you to come live with us."

That day I started to believe in life again. Maybe there was hope for me after all.

In fact, it was because of what Katie's parents did for me that I decided to pursue a career in children's social services. I wanted to work with orphaned children—children who I understood. I wanted them to know they weren't alone, and they were still loved. They weren't outcasts and they still had their entire lives ahead of them.

The sound of a door opening alerted me to the present.

"Oh.em.gee!" I squealed as Katie emerged from her bridal suite. "Katie, you look absolutely stunning. Greg is going to pass out when he sees you!"

"He better not," she chuckled. "I'm not sure Jamie could catch Greg's ass if he goes down."

"Speaking of this notorious Jamie . . . what kind of best man misses the rehearsal?" I question. "Seems pretty lame if you ask me."

"It's not a big deal, Ireland," she assured me. "And, you're right. No one asked you," she added, nudging me in the ribs.

"It might be your wedding day, but don't be a bitch," I said, trying to hide my smile.

"Whatever! You're just lucky I'm not a Bridezilla like those girls in that crazy TV show!" she sassed. "Really though, like I said, it's not a big deal. He had some big corporate function last night and apologized profusely to Greg and me."

"Still seems like a lame excuse to me," I quipped. "What does this guy do again?"

"He's Greg's partner at the architectural firm here in Detroit. You know—Roberts, McMillan & Associates? How do you not know any of this?"

"Oh, well I knew Greg owned the architectural firm with someone. I guess I just never realized that his business partner was his best friend and his best man. I guess I just assumed it was some old guy who had a perma pole stuck up his stiff ass. If he's Greg's best friend, then why have I never met him? They've been partners for a while, right?"

"Yeah, well he is and I guess they're in some bidding war with another company on a pretty big project in the city. So, that's where he was last night—rubbing elbows with corporate bigwigs so their company would get the project. It's really not a big deal. Besides, it's not like Greg could very well go in his place and one of them had to be there in order to help pay for this wedding. So, really, he did me a favor," Katie explained.

"And, all he has to do is escort you down the aisle, hold my ring and give a speech at the reception—easy peasy, right?" she rambled. "And, Jamie never came out with us because he was married. He and his wife just recently divorced. Thank god for Jamie really. Staci's a real twat. I do feel sorry for their son, Tanner, though. He's in middle school and doesn't need his parents' bullshit piled on his shoulders."

I hardly heard a word Katie said after architect. My mind immediately drifted to Bentley begging me to play Legos or Tinkertoys with him.

"Please, Shamrock," he begged. "I'm sick of playing dress up. I want to build something cool. Build the tallest skyscraper with me."

Off in the distance I heard Katie clearing her throat, bringing me back to the present. "Ireland, did you hear a word I just said?" she asked with a hint of annoyance in her voice. "You need to get your head in the game!"

"Uhhhh, right. Yeah, whatever you say. I guess if you don't care then I should cut the guy some slack."

"Where do you keep drifting off to?" she asked.

"Just thinking about someone. It doesn't matter."

"Just someone, or him? And, by the look on your face and the unshed tears in your eyes it most certainly doesn't look like it doesn't matter. Talk to me, Ireland."

"Just drop it, Katie. Not today—today is about you. Now let's go meet this mysterious Jamie and get you married to your Prince Charming."

"Pffft," she laughed. "We both certainly know that Greg will never be Prince Charming, but he certainly does try and I love him for it."

"You're such a sap," I teased as we walked to the church's vestibule, stopping to continue our conversation. "I can't believe you're leaving me all alone in the world of Singledom."

"Oh come on. We both knew that Greg had to put a ring on it eventually. We've been together over a decade. We're in our thirties for god's sake—that's practically forty!" she exclaimed.

"Thanks! Way to make me feel even better about myself," I said, rolling my eyes at her. "Maybe I should leave the reception early so I can head to the animal shelter and pick up a cat . . . or two."

"Shut up! Oh, but if you do get cats, make sure they are gangster kitties and name them Bonnie and Clyde!" she exclaimed, clapping her hands together. "Oh, I changed my mind—Thelma and Louise!"

"Oh my god. You've actually put thought into this. I'm destined to live the life of a cat lady," I sighed, shaking my head.

"Of course, I've thought about it. Mom and I have actually had several conversations about this. She wanted to get you into counseling back in college, but I talked her out of it and convinced her that you were actually seeing someone. You can thank me later," she said with a wink.

"You've got to be kidding. You've talked about this with Shannon?" I screeched.

"What? Don't act so surprised. You know I don't hide anything from my mother. Well, except for the fact that her baby girl isn't walking down this aisle with her cherry intact," she giggled. "Besides, it's not like you're actually willing to date anyone. I've known you for nearly twenty years, Ireland. You haven't had one serious relationship. If you weren't fucking and chucking 'em, I'd think you were sexually impaired, or something," she said, eyeing me up and down.

"We're not continuing this conversation right now. Let's go and get you hitched. Oh, and for the record—your mother caught you and Greg screwing like rabbits about five years ago. She came to me in tears and I talked her off the ledge. I told her you were a smart kid and were using protection . . . blah, blah, blah. She was so embarrassed. She begged me to never tell you," I said, opening the doors into the vestibule where the rest of the bridal party minus Greg was waiting. I turned back to find Katie's jaw nearly hitting the floor. "So, I guess you'll actually be the one thanking me later," I said, grinning.

As I pulled a stunned Katie through the vestibule doors, I spotted him. Our eyes locked and I felt all the blood rush to my head.

"Whoa, Ireland! Are you OK?" Katie asked frantically. "You look like you've seen a ghost! You need to sit down before you pass out. I already have to worry about Greg collapsing at the altar, I can't very well worry about you now, too."

"I'll be fine. Who . . . Who's that guy standing over there chatting with your brother?" I asked with a quiver in my voice.

"Oh, that's Jamie. Why? Do you know him?" She questioned.

"Are you sure? It looks like . . . are you sure that's Jamie?" I asked, confusedly.

"Yes, I'm sure. He's Greg's best friend. I'm pretty sure I

would know my future husband's best friend. Why? What the hell is going on with you right now? You're scaring me," she nearly screamed.

"Shhhh. Stop yelling. People are going to start looking. He's going to come over here."

"Of course, people are going to start looking, Ireland. It's my wedding and you're my maid of honor. We're going to be front and center here in a minute and I hate to break it to you, but he's the one walking you down the aisle."

I took a few deep breaths and convinced myself that the wedding just had me in a nostalgic mood and I was seeing things. There was no way that Jamie was Bentley—none. After all, we both lived in Nashville as kids not in Michigan. Why would Bentley be an architect in Detroit? What are the odds of us both ending up in the same place—over five hundred miles away from where our story began?

"Is everything all right over here," Jamie asked, walking over toward us. "Katie, my best friend sure is one lucky man. You look beautiful."

"Thank you, Jamie," she said, wrapping her arms around his shoulders and pulling him in for a warm embrace and a gentle peck on the cheek.

"Jamie, this is my best friend and maid of honor—Ireland."

Recognition swept across his face at the sound of my name. "Ireland? That's a pretty uncommon name?" he mumbled.

"Yeah, my mom was pretty much obsessed with the Emerald Isle. I guess I should be thankful that she didn't name me after the Blarney Stone," I chuckled, weakly.

"I knew an Ireland once, back when I lived in Nashville," he began to explain. "I haven't seen her in almost twenty years though. She had to move away suddenly," he continued, lost in his own memories. "I'm sorry. I don't mean to ramble. I'm sure I'm boring the two of you."

That's when the pieces began to come together—*Roberts,*

Nashville, architect . . .

"That's ironic," Katie interrupted. "Ireland is originally from Nashville, too. Do you two know each other?"

"Bentley?" I asked, swallowing back the lump in my throat. "Bentley—Is it really you?"

"Shamrock? Those eyes—I knew those were my girl's eyes," he said, pulling me into his well-defined chest. Even under his crisp, white button-down, I could make out his well-defined six pack.

"I never thought I'd see you again," I whispered into his ear.

"I've missed you," he said, planting a kiss on the side of my cheek. His breath on my skin sending a shiver up my spine.

"Bentley?" Katie questioned, her eyes widening as recognition set in. "As in THE Bentley?"

I just stared back at her, hoping my eyes would tell her I would answer her questions later.

"Yes, Katie, I am THE Bentley," Jamie explained. "At least I hope I am anyways. And, I also hope you've only heard good stories."

"OK, but I'm still confused. Why have we only known you as Jamie? Are you in the Witness Protection Program? Oh dear god—are you in the mafia? Is my wedding going to be under siege?"

"While that would be a much better story, you can relax Katie, I'm not in the mafia and your wedding will not be under government attack," he chuckled, rubbing her on the shoulder. "Actually, it's pretty simple, and not that exciting of a story, really. My middle name is Bentley. I was named after my Uncle James and everyone in my family called me by my middle name so we wouldn't be confused. He was my role model growing up. I wanted to be an architect just like him.

"After the accident," Bentley paused, looking toward me as if asking for my permission to continue. I nodded before he proceeded. "When he died, I decided I'd begin using my first name as a tribute to him. His connection has also worked to my advantage in my career. My uncle was highly regarded during his time as an architect."

"Oh, OK," Katie responded, biting her bottom lip. "Well look at me asking too many questions and making everyone uncomfortable. I'm going to go check my lipstick one more time and then we can get this show on the road."

"I think I'll come help you," I told Katie, excusing myself to Bentley. *I hope he didn't really expect me to call him Jamie. He would always be my Bentley—my one and only.*

"Are you OK?" she asked as we walked toward the ladies' room.

"I'm going to have to be, aren't I?"

Chapter Two

BENTLEY AND I first met when I was seven and he was nine. It was during my Aunt Char's wedding. Bentley, my new Uncle James' nephew, had the honor of being ring bearer while I was the flower girl. The dress I wore was made of white satin with pink trim and resembled Aunt Char's gown. A second skirt of white tulle under the satin dress made it nearly impossible for me to sit without drowning in a sea of fabric. Thinking back on it, I'm fairly positive that I looked like the little girl version of the Stay Puft Marshmallow Man.

I remember my hair bouncing up and down in the tightest ringlets under a crown of white roses and baby's breath. At the rehearsal dinner the night before, my aunt and new uncle had given me a silver chain with an attached arrow pendant to wear around my neck. It's something I still wear daily—attached to the same silver chain with the locket Bentley had given me on my tenth birthday. That chain, the two pictures secured in the tiny locket, and my mother's Claddagh ring that my father had given her when he proposed were all I had left from any of them. Those three pieces of jewelry are all that remain from my former life—a life that I so desperately wish was still mine. I wear them all, closely tucked near my heart.

"Mommy, these curls are making my head hurt," I complained, twirling them into an even tighter circle around my middle finger.

"Ireland, stop fussing. Are you ready to do the most important job? Your Aunt Char is counting on you."

"Yes, I'm ready, but do I really have to walk with a boy? All the boys at school have cooties. I'm sure this one does, too," I whined to my mother.

"Ireland, I assure you that boys don't have cooties. One day, a VERY long time from now, I'll be helping you get ready on your wedding day—to a boy," she chuckled, reaching out to tickle my sides.

"Ewww, Mommy, that's gross. Besides, if boys don't have cooties then why don't I have a daddy?"

"Ireland, stop it! You know you have a father!" she exclaimed with a hint of desperation in her voice.

"I know you don't remember much about him, but you do have a daddy. He's just in heaven. But, he loved you so much, darling. So much. I'm sure he's watching down on us today with that big, ol' dopey grin on his face," she continued, before pausing to wipe a stray tear from her cheek. "But, no more sad tears today, right? He'd only want us to cry happy tears."

"OK, Mommy," I said. "But, will you tell me more about him—about Daddy?"

"Your Daddy was a hero, Ireland. Of course I'll tell you all about him, but first we need to get to a wedding," she insisted. "Let's get you down that aisle, shall we? We don't want to leave your Aunt Char waiting."

My dad died when I was just a little over two years old. He was an officer for the Nashville Police Department and was killed during a routine traffic stop when a drunk driver slammed into him as he was issuing a ticket on the side of the interstate. The only memories of him came from stories that my mother shared with me before her own tragic death.

I remember seeing a few pictures of him cradling me as a newborn. But, a weathered photo of him holding me just a few weeks before his death would forever remain engraved in my mind. I'd been sick, probably with one of those nagging ear infections I'd often suffered as a toddler. My cheeks were tear-stained, my eyes swollen and my nose chapped and reddened.

Snuggled up on my dad's bare chest, I wore flannel, pink-footed pajamas with my favorite, green checkered blanket resting against my back. If I closed my eyes tight enough, I could almost feel the back of his hand resting gently across my cheek and the smell of his rugged, woodsy aftershave. I couldn't be sure if it was really my dad's scent I was remembering, or just the way I always imagined he would have smelled.

I'd do anything to have that photograph now, but after my mother was killed all our stuff just vanished. I was never able to collect my keepsakes such as my green checkered blanket, the box of photographs from my parents' wedding or any other items left of my childhood.

A BASKET FILLED to the brim with white rose petals was waiting for me as my mother and I entered the church antechamber. From inside the church, I could hear the faint hum of violins over the soft whispers of the guests. There was a nervous energy filling the room as the bridesmaids and groomsmen began to take their places.

It was as if a sea of rosy pink had exploded around me. Even the men were dressed in white tuxedos with thick pink belts wrapped around their waists, a color reminding me of the medicine my mother had given me last week when I woke up complaining of an upset tummy.

"You need to stand here right behind me, Ireland. I'm going to walk up the aisle first and then you'll follow behind me just like we practiced last night, OK?"

"OK," I nodded, as I noticed a boy, about my age, standing alone in the corner playing with a Game Boy. He was wearing the same matching white tuxedo as the older men.

I stepped out of my place in line and went over to him.

"Are you the ring bearer? The boy who will be walking with me down the aisle?" I asked.

He looked up briefly from the electronic game. "Yep, I guess that's me," he said, before lowering his head.

"I'm Ireland. What's your name?"

"That's a funny name," he said without raising his head. "And, I'm James, but everyone calls me Bentley. It's my middle name."

"Humph, well Bentley, you aren't very nice." I responded with a scowl. "I think my mommy is wrong. I think you probably do have cooties."

He looked up at me and I actually saw hurt in his brown eyes. They were the color of Hershey Kisses—my favorite candy. Maybe this boy wasn't so bad after all. I was willing to give him another chance.

"I'm named after the country," I explained. "My daddy was Irish and my mommy loves telling me stories about my heritage. She's even told me stories about giants living in Ireland once. Isn't that cool," I said. "What game are you playing?"

"I'm playing Tetris and you sure do talk a lot."

"I'm sorry. I just want to get to know you better. My mommy told me that once Aunt Char and James get married we'll be like family. She told me to be nice. So, I'm being nice," I giggled. "Mommy plays that Tetris game on my big Nintendo that's hooked up to the TV. She really likes that Zelda game, too. I really only like my Barbie game and the Chip 'n Dales Rescue Rangers game. Have you played those before?"

"No!" he shouted, causing me to grimace.

"What's wrong?" I asked.

"You! You ask too many questions. I lost my concentration and lost my game. I was on level fourteen, too. That's the highest I've ever gotten and you had to go and ruin it!" he yelled, stomping his foot.

"I—I'm sorry," I cried, sniffing my nose. "I didn't mean to upset you. I'll leave you alone from now on. I won't bother you anymore. I just—I just thought we could be friends—that's all."

Bentley looked into my eyes and I actually saw a hint of remorse. "Don't cry, Shamrock. I'm sorry for making you cry. Please don't cry. I *shouldn't have taken it out on you," he said, extending his shirt sleeve for me to wipe away my tears.*

"Why—why did you call me Shamrock," I asked, as my tears began to subside.

"Don't they have lots of shamrocks in Ireland?" he answered with a dimpled-grin on his face.

Just then my mom came over and ushered us to our place in line.

"THAT'S OUR CUE, Ireland." Bentley said, snapping his fingers in front of my face.

"What?" I responded, shaking my head in confusion.

"We need to go down the aisle. It's our turn," he whispered. "And, by the scowl on Katie's face she's going to kick our asses if we don't go right now."

I quickly turned to see what Bentley was talking about and chuckled when I saw Katie's signature, bitch glare.

"You know you love me," I mouthed, blowing her a kiss.

"I'll love you even more when you're walking down that damn aisle," she mouthed back.

I was so stunned after seeing Bentley after nearly two decades that I hadn't really gotten a good look at him. Now here I stood, only twenty feet away and I couldn't help but take him all in. I always had a schoolgirl crush on him, but staring at the grown up version of Bentley was doing things to me that I hadn't felt in a long time, if ever. He looked debonair in his black tuxedo—his broad shoulders and muscular chest filling out his coat perfectly.

The wine-colored tie and vest that Katie had chosen for the groomsmen only enhanced the amber flecks in his smoldering, chocolaty eyes. His brown hair was short, yet just long enough to slick back with a tiny amount of gel. His day-old scruff outlining his chiseled jaw left me with goosebumps as I imagined what it would feel like if he were to pepper a trail of heated kisses down my naked body.

When he kissed me on the cheek earlier, I wantonly breathed in the smell of his cologne radiating off his lapel. It was a mix of lemon zest with a hint of vanilla. Why did I have an almost immediate urge to ask him what he was wearing? It's not like I needed a mental inventory of what to buy him for Christmas. Bentley will be gone again after this weekend, and things will return to normal as if we hadn't just run into each other again after nearly twenty years.

"Earth to Ireland," Katie said, breaking through my thoughts.

"Shit. Sorry. Shit—I just swore in church. Shit," I stammered.

"Snap out of it. Will you, please?" she demanded sternly before continuing. "I need Greg's ring. And wipe the drool from your chin."

I looked at her with wide eyes before handing her the titanium band. "Seriously? I was drooling?" I questioned.

"No, but you very well could've been with that dopey smile on your sex-flushed face," she whisper-yelled. "Now would you pay attention to me—your best friend? It is MY wedding day after all."

Chapter Three

GREG'S NIECE AND nephew were twirling around the dance floor to "(I've Had) The Time of My Life" pretending to be Baby and Johnny out on the dance floor. I was almost certain it was Katie who had played *Dirty Dancing* for the kids a time or two. She'd been obsessed with that movie since before we'd even met.

When she told me she was marrying Greg, I was actually terrified that she was going to make the entire bridal party learn the movie's closing routine complete with the deadlift jump. Thank god she'd never approached me with the idea and I definitely wasn't going to give her the suggestion. I'd seen all of those videos trending on YouTube with the bridal party learning iconic eighties numbers and the last thing I wanted was for my uncoordinated ass to be plastered on the Internet for all eternity.

As engrossed as I was watching Greg's niece and nephew, I didn't notice anyone approaching me from behind.

"Care to dance?" Bentley whispered, placing his arms around my shoulders and pulling me into him. I quickly stepped out of his embrace, not wanting myself to so easily fall into the comfort he was offering me.

"Shit!" I said, punching him in the arm. "Don't do that again, you scared me."

"Sorry, I forgot my Shamrock was really more of a pansy,"

he said with a chuckle.

"I see you haven't changed at all. Still the same smart ass you were as a teenager," I said, not humored at his attempt at sarcasm.

"You're confusing me, Shamrock."

"Why am I confusing you?" I snapped.

"For starters you need to lighten up a bit," he suggested, rolling his eyes. "And, secondly, you're confusing me because I noticed you staring at me—your eyes practically devouring me during the ceremony. But since then you've avoided me like the plague. And, now I ask you to dance and instead of falling into my arms you recoil like I'm a snake. What gives, Ireland?"

I sighed, knowing that he'd eventually want answers.

"I'm not avoiding you and I definitely wasn't staring. I see we can add vanity to your list of attributes," I said, straight-faced.

"Seriously, Shamrock, stop the charade," he pleaded. "I know you. This girl isn't you. And, I know Katie well enough to know that her best friend wouldn't be a first class bitch."

I stopped at his words. He was right; I was putting up a front. I had to shut him out now, or run the risk of losing him all over again. I already lost him once before, and I think I'd crumble if I had to go through that pain and torment again.

"I guess you're going for the silent treatment now, huh? Oh wait, I remember now, you're more of a *Flashdance* girl, aren't you? Why didn't you just say something? I'm sure I can request a song," he said with a knowing smirk.

"Oh my god! Isn't that what we danced to at my Aunt Char's wedding? I can't believe you actually remember that," I chuckled. "You wanted nothing to do with me. You were dancing so far away from me that a third person could have been between us. You didn't even want to hold my hands!"

"Yeah, I guess it took me awhile to realize how great you were," he said with a wink.

Without even thinking, I put my hand to my neck and began

fingering my heart-shaped locket. It had always provided me with comfort when I'd been in an uneasy situation.

"Is that—is that what I think it is?" Bentley questioned, before reaching out and placing three fingers on my chest.

My breath hitched at his touch. I said a silent prayer that he hadn't noticed. He moved his fingers and placed them over mine on the locket.

"Relax, Ireland. It's just me," he whispered, as he opened the locket to reveal the two photographs I kept tucked safely inside. On the left was a picture of my mother and me during my Aunt Char's wedding reception. She'd picked me up and was twirling me around the dance floor when my Uncle James had captured the moment. On the right side was a picture of Bentley and me on the day we'd finished the tree house behind his parents' cabin in the Smokies.

"You still wear this?" he questioned.

"Every day," I whispered, holding back the tears that were just beginning to well up.

"I'm sorry, Bentley, but I can't do this. Not tonight—maybe not ever," I said, as I turned to walk away.

"Don't run again, Ireland," Bentley said, grabbing me by the shoulders.

"Run?" I practically seethed. "You think I ran? I didn't have a choice, Bentley! They took me away. I didn't have anywhere to go. I had to leave."

"You could have stayed with us. I told you before the funeral that you could stay with us."

"Bentley, we were kids. We couldn't make those kinds of decisions. There were laws—formalities."

"But, my parents said you could've come with us. We looked for you for months. After you left, I begged them to find you. You may not realize it, but I lost everything that day, too, Ireland. Uncle James was my best friend—my role model. And, you—you were My Everything. Even at sixteen, I thought the sun rose and set by you. I loved you, Shamrock," he admitted, his frustration only growing with each word he spoke.

My ears began to ring. Surely it was the loud jazz music coming from the ballroom. I must be hearing things. There is no way that Bentley just told me that he'd loved me.

"Did you hear me, Ireland? I said I loved you."

"Ye—yes, I heard you," I stuttered, shakily. "But, why? Why are you telling me this now? I don't even know who you are anymore. You have a successful career, a wife—a son. And, me. I'm not the same fourteen-year-old girl who you loved, Bentley. I'm a thirty-two-year-old woman with eighteen years of baggage."

Taking his finger, he tucked a fallen piece of blond hair behind the gardenia that was fastened behind my ear. He moved in so closely I could feel his breath with each word he spoke. "I'm telling you because I've missed you, Shamrock. Not a day's gone by in those eighteen years when I haven't thought about you. You were even on my mind the day I married my ex-wife."

I gasped at his admission.

"That's right. I loved Staci, but I caught myself remembering you on my wedding day. Maybe that's why the marriage was doomed before it even began. Maybe I didn't give her the kind of attention a husband should give his wife. Maybe that's why she sought out the love of other men and cheated on me more times than I care to discuss right now," he huffed.

"I'll never regret being with her because I have Tanner, but you must know she's in the past, Ireland. So, how's that for eighteen years of baggage?" he continued, rubbing the creases in his forehead. I didn't notice the faint lines before, but in my opinion they didn't make him look older. They made him look wiser and more mature than the carefree Bentley from all those years ago. I'm sure each line told a story, and in that moment I found myself wanting to know about each one—all eighteen years' worth.

"I—I didn't realize. I don't know what to say."

"You don't have to say anything right now, but just know I'm not letting this go. I'm not letting you walk away. Not this time," he said with confidence as he quickly turned and left me alone once again on the dance floor. I guess this time he was the one to walk away.

The music stopped as Katie hobbled off the dance floor and headed my way.

"What'd he say to you? He's upset you, hasn't he?" she asked, pointing toward Bentley. "I'm so sorry, Ireland. If I'd had known that Jamie was THE Bentley then Greg and I would've never asked him to be in the wedding. You know that, right. You're my best friend—practically my sister—and I'd never want to hurt you and jeopardize our relationship."

"I'm fine. He didn't say anything that wasn't true," I sighed. "But, this conversation, is for another day—we'll make it a girls' day when you get back from Bora Bora. I'll tell you all about my troubles then. Maybe I'll even come to your office and lie on your massive couch."

"You don't pay me enough to be able to sleep on my couch," she sassed.

"You're right, my friendship is the only payment you need. And we're changing the subject, so tell me why you're walking like your eighty-year-old grandmother?"

"Pfft. Have you seen Doris bust a move on the dance floor tonight? Ever since she got her knees and hips done she's been a beast. I wish I could fly around like she does."

"Yeah, I did," I chuckled. "She had Bentley out there doing the Cha-Cha Slide. I thought he was going to wave his white flag if she'd kept going. Seriously though, are you OK? You look like you're about to die. The Grumpy Cat scowl on your face doesn't scream blushing bride."

"Yeah, my feet are just killing me. Whoever told me to buy the four-inch stilettos needs to be punched in the throat," she said, glaring at me. "Oh wait! That was you! 'They're cute,' you said. 'Think about how they'll look in the air and wrapped around your husband's neck,' you said. I think you forgot to factor in how miserable I would be and how much I really enjoy my Tieks."

"You done?"

"What? Tieks even came out with a new bridal line!" she huffed.

"No? How 'bout now? You done now?"

"Fine, but these damn things are going in the garbage in the morning. I do fully intend to make use of them tonight, though."

"See! You can't deny the fact that you're already wet thinking about seeing those resting on Greg's shoulders as he eats at your buffet later. Am I right?" I said, nudging her in the shoulder.

We were both doubled over in laughter when Bentley and Greg approached us from behind.

Bentley put his arm around my shoulder and pulled me close.

"You're dancing with me this time. I'm not taking no for an answer so don't even try to pull away," he stated gruffly into my ear. Before I even had time to respond, the DJ began announcing the next song.

"This song goes out to tonight's maid of honor from the best man," he said over the loudspeaker. "Shamrock, here's to reconnecting, second chances, and never having to say goodbye."

I heard just the first few beats of Meghan Trainor's and John Legend's duet, "Like I'm Gonna Lose You," and the tears began. The song fit us like a glove—like it was written just for the two of us.

Bentley pulled me into his chest and wiped my tears with his thumb.

"I thought when you walked away earlier that we were done," I whispered.

"I was giving you some time—some space. I know seeing

each other after all the years has been difficult for you. Shit, it's been difficult for me. But, I'd be lying if I said I didn't feel an immediate connection with you. I'm drawn to you, Shamrock. Please say you'll dance with me?"

"I didn't think you were giving me a choice," I teased. "But if you're really giving me the option . . ." I added with a wink.

"Yeah, I'm not. Especially since you're toying with me now. Do you see what you're doing to me?" he said, nodding down at his fully aroused state.

I gasped at his candidness. "Bentley!"

Bentley released me from his hold and grabbed my hands so there was at least some space between us.

"Don't make me apologize for wanting you, Shamrock. I'm a man—a man with needs—and you're fucking gorgeous. I always thought you were pretty, but fuck . . ." he trailed off, as he began eyeing me up and down as if he were a lion and I his prey.

I stood there speechless for a moment. "The song is almost over. Maybe we should just actually dance since you went to the trouble of requesting it for me," I finally suggested.

"I think you're right," he agreed, pulling me toward the dance floor.

Once we'd secured our place among the other couples, he brought me to his chest once again. His fingers rubbed up and down my spine as I placed my cheek against his chest. The sound of Bentley's heart beating was a reminder that he was here with me and I couldn't be afraid to lose him—like I seemed to lose everyone that I've ever cared about.

The song ended, but we held each other for a few more beats. I tried pulling away, but instead he cupped the side of my face and looked deep into my soul. Without hesitation, Bentley lightly brushed his lips against mine. His lips tasted like the champagne we'd both been drinking throughout the night. I suddenly craved more and I wasn't talking about the bubbly. I needed more Bentley.

I hummed, virtually giving him the go-ahead to deepen the kiss. He moved without hesitation as he nipped on my lower lip before parting my seam with a flick of his tongue. Our tongues danced to the rhythm of the next song and I could feel his arousal only grow against my stomach. His lips were searing mine. The kiss was deep and passionate as if he were branding me—marking me as his own.

With his kiss, I was transported back in time when Bentley and I first kissed—only I was twelve then and we were experimenting in his tree house.

We'd spent three summers designing and constructing the tree house with a lot of extra help from Uncle James. Bentley's family had a cabin in the Smoky Mountains near Gatlinburg and my mom and I often visited when my Aunt Char and Uncle James would stay.

"Bentley, why does this sign say no girls allowed?" I asked, ripping the sign down as I crouched down so I wouldn't hit my head on the low-hanging piece of tree bark. "I'm a girl and I helped you build this thing. Are we not friends anymore?"

"You're not a girl. You don't count, Shamrock."

"I am too a girl," I yelled.

"Well you aren't one of THOSE girls."

"And who are THOSE girls?" I questioned.

"All of the girls at school want to hold hands and kiss and stuff. You aren't like that, Shamrock."

I sighed for a minute. I was like that—I just couldn't tell him. I really liked Bentley, but I didn't want to lose my best friend. I guess this was my chance. It was now or never.

"But . . ." I paused.

"But what, Shamrock? Spill it. No secrets between us, remember?"

"Yes, I remember," I said, hesitantly. "But, what if I wanted to kiss you?"

"Do you want to kiss me?"

I needed to tell him the truth—it was now or never. "Yes," I said, blinking rapidly so I could avoid looking him in the eyes.

"I've waited forever to hear you say that," he sighed in relief, before coming in and planting the wettest, sloppiest kiss on my lips.

I squirmed with the sudden invasion of his lips on mine and fell backwards onto the floor boards. I bumped my head and the walls of the tree house began spinning around me. I tried to sit up but my pony-tail holder got caught around one of the nails in the floor. If I'd fallen on it any harder, it probably would've pierced my skin. Bentley put his hand behind my head and tried unhooking my hair tie, but his thumb managed to pick up a splinter in the process. He was finally able to get me down the ladder and back to the cabin where his mom was able to remove the splinter wedged in his thumb.

Because of my fall, my mom insisted on taking me to the hospital. I had to spend the evening in the emergency room where I was treated for a concussion. I remember Bentley sat by my bed holding my hand the entire time, saying he would never try and kiss me again. I knew I didn't want that, but I did think that whoever thought first kisses were magical was sadly mistaken.

I chuckled to myself before Bentley pulled away. He left me breathless and I immediately yearned for his warm lips against mine.

"I know you aren't actually laughing because there's nothing to laugh about here," he said, with a hint of annoyance in his voice.

"Oh, I'm most definitely not laughing at what just happened. No, that—that was definitely magical unlike our first kiss. Do you remember that afternoon in the tree house?"

He laughed, "How could I forget? I do believe I said I would never kiss you again."

"It didn't take you long to break that promise," I reminded him. "I'm pretty sure you were kissing me again the next day."

"I was and if I recall it got better with each kiss," he said, pecking me on the nose before he twirled me around and dipped me. For a moment, it was like we were the only ones on the dance floor.

The lights brightened, reminding us that we weren't in fact alone. I looked over and saw Katie in the middle of a conversation with her not-so-favorite aunt.

"I think maid of honor duty calls," I said, pointing in Katie's direction. "It looks like she needs saving from an awkward conversation. I'll see you later?"

"You can count on it, Shamrock," Bentley said, taking my hand and kissing it lightly.

I turned and walked away stopping to take a quick peek behind my shoulder. Bentley was watching me walk away and as I turned he blew a kiss in my direction. I swiveled on my heels and tossed my hands in the air to capture his kiss in my palm. I held it against my chest for a minute before blowing one back in his direction just as we'd done as kids. I couldn't help the butterflies that were swirling around inside me. Bentley was affecting me, whether I wanted him to or not.

"OH MY GOD, you really saved my ass out there," Katie said as we walked toward the photo booth. "Aunt Genevieve was going on and on about her gout. I swear I threw up in my mouth. I was worried next she was going to tell me about the most effective brand of hemorrhoid cream."

I snorted from my hysterical laughter. "I—I can't even," I giggled as we both entered the booth.

"What? You know it's true," she exclaimed, draping a bright pink, feather boa around her neck.

"OK, moving on," I laughed. "How do these look? Do they make my nose look big?" I asked of the ginormous plastic glasses I'd put on my face.

"Beautiful as always, darling!"

Katie and I tried on various accessories from shiny beads to glittery masquerade masks and plastic mustaches. We were gig-gling so hard at all the photos being printed inside that we didn't even hear Greg and Bentley enter the booth behind us.

"Boo!" they shouted in unison, causing us both to jump.

"Eeeek," Katie screamed, jumping out of her seat. "Don't do that again. I almost peed myself and I'm not wearing any underwear under this thing."

"You're not?" Greg said, his eyes bulging out of his head. "I think I need to further inspect this situation," he added, bending over to grab the hem of Katie's dress. Bentley and I turned to look at each other with horror written on our faces.

"What do we do?" I mouthed.

"I have no idea because they're blocking our exit," he responded, sounding a little panicked.

Katie burst into a fit of laughter. "Would you all calm down! Of course I'm wearing underwear. And, Gregory, stop trying to lift up my skirt. No one wants to see the granny panties that I actually have hiding under here!"

"Ugh. Way to ruin it for me, Katie," Greg groaned. "You couldn't just let me pretend you were going commando under there. That would have been epic."

"You know what else would be epic? The groom sleeping alone on his wedding night," she deadpanned.

The look on Greg's face was priceless. "Oh snap! She got you, Gregory!" I giggled, fist bumping my best friend.

"Something tells me you don't actually mean that," Greg said, capturing Katie's lips.

"Seriously, you two need to get a room," Bentley piped in.

"I think we're gonna sneak off for a bit. You two cover for us," Greg said with a wink, picking Katie up and carrying her out of the photo booth.

"Those two really are perfect for each other," Bentley said, surprising me.

"Bentley Roberts, you sound like such a hopeless romantic."

"I guess I can be. It's just nice to see them happy," he said, placing a top hat on his head.

"Looks good on you, but I think you should try the cowboy hat on instead," I suggested.

"Yeah? Wanna ride a cowboy, huh?" he said, pulling me down onto his lap and placing the cowboy hat on my head.

The light from the camera's flash blinked once as Bentley captured my mouth with his.

I giggled, pulling away from his embrace. If I kept allowing him to kiss me like that I wasn't sure I'd be able to keep controlling myself around him.

"That's hardly what I said and you know it," I added in mock disgust.

"I can't help that my ears only hear what they want to hear," he shrugged, innocently.

We spent the next several minutes in the booth making goofy faces as the camera captured every moment of our reunion. I pulled the strip of photos out of the printer and hardly had a chance to look at them before Bentley pulled them from my grip.

"Can I have those?" he asked.

"Sure. But why?"

"It's not important why. I just want to remember this moment. That's all. Hopeless romantic—remember?"

"Right," I sighed. "We should probably get out of here though. I think there are people waiting to get in here to take their picture for the album."

Nearing midnight, the wedding reception was coming to an end.

"I guess it's time to say goodbye. I need to see if Katie needs anything," I said, exiting the photo booth.

"Meet me at the bottom of the stairs after Greg and Katie leave," Bentley requested. "I'm not ready to say goodbye to you. Not yet."

"Bentley, I can't. Trust me, I want to, but my heart and my head are in two very different places right now."

"Then I'll see you tomorrow, right? At Greg and Katie's farewell brunch? They're supposed to open gifts and then we're to see them off to Bora Bora. I already told Greg I'd be there. Say you'll come with me and then we can go grab coffee and talk."

"Yeah, I'll be there. But, I think I should just go home after brunch."

"It's just coffee, Shamrock. Not sex. Although it can be sex if you want it to be."

I just stared at him with my mouth agape.

"Relax, Ireland. I'm not an asshole. I was only kidding. Just coffee—I swear. No funny business."

"OK, tomorrow then. Just coffee," I repeated, before turning to find Katie.

"Just coffee," I reminded myself once more.

I stopped Katie and Greg at the top of the stairs before they headed down to grab the limo.

"I love you both," I said, as I gave them both quick hugs.

"We love you, too. Where's Bentley," Katie asked, raising her eyebrow.

"I don't know. I left him a few minutes ago on the dance floor and I told him I would see him in the morning at your brunch."

"Really?" she questioned

"Yes, really. What do you think I am? A whore?"

"Um, do you really want me to answer that?"

"You're a bitch," I quipped.

"You can't call me a bitch. It's my wedding day."

"Actually, it's past midnight so your wedding day is technically over."

"Touché. And, for the record, I don't actually think you're a whore. I just thought you'd want to spend more time talking with him. That's all."

"We're going to get coffee in the afternoon. But, enough

about me. You two have a honeymoon suite with your name on it. We'll talk later."

"Are you sure?"

"GO! I'm not telling you again."

"Fine, but I need to toss the bouquet. I forgot to do it while we were still inside."

The crowd of guests began to gather at the bottom of the stairs with their streamers in hand.

"OK, I'll let everyone know. Give me a few minutes to run down the back steps."

I made it to the crowd of people and signaled Katie with the go-ahead. Greg made a quick speech thanking everyone for coming as Katie turned around and tossed the bouquet of roses into the crowd below. A few women lunged to catch it, causing it to bounce into the air and land a few feet behind them—right at my feet.

I looked down at the ground and immediately felt his presence behind me once again.

"Are you going to pick that up," he asked, his husky voice sending a chill through my body.

Chapter Four

MY ALARM BUZZED at seven o'clock and I slammed my head against the pillow in frustration. It was far too early, especially for a Sunday. My head was pounding and the sunlight streaming in through the crack in my mini blinds only worsened the already splitting migraine. I needed coffee and I needed it stat. Katie was really going to hear an earful from me for scheduling her damn brunch gathering so early. Who schedules a brunch for eight o'clock in the morning anyways? Isn't that really just breakfast?

The eight glasses of champagne I'd drunk during the reception coupled with my fitful sleep had really left me in a bad situation this morning. I tossed and turned for several hours thinking about my last conversation with Bentley as well as what the afternoon had in store for us. I sighed and sat up too quickly. The room started to spin and I quickly rested my head back against the pillow. I'd just close my eyes for a few more minutes.

"No, I'm not picking that up! Have you lost your damn mind? Katie even agreed with me this morning while we were getting her ready to walk down the aisle. I'm destined to be a cat lady," I told Bentley.

"The Cat Lady, huh? I always pictured you as more of a dog girl myself."

"Ugh. No dogs. You have to take those out and walk them. Cats just shit in a box."

"You really are crazy, Shamrock. I don't remember this side of you," he chuckled. "How about you humor me and pick it up anyways before the bunch of wide-eyed, wild chicks come and tackle us. Because this old man left his football playing days behind him at the University of Tennessee over a decade ago," Bentley added, pointing at the bridesmaids who'd been previously lunging for the bouquet.

"Fine," I huffed, bending over to pick up the bouquet of roses. "But, this certainly doesn't mean anything. I'm definitely not the next girl at this wedding getting married—in fact I'm never setting myself up for that kind of loss."

"What does that mean?" he inquired, with concern written all over his face. "When we were younger you were always so excited by the idea of getting married. I remember being so thankful when you finally grew out of the dress-up phase. But, to be honest, after a few months, I actually kind of missed it."

I smiled at his admission. "You did, huh? You were always so handsome in that denim vest of yours."

"I did look rather dapper, didn't I?" he answered with a wink. "But, don't try to schmooze me by evading my question, Ireland. Do you really feel like you'll never get married? Are you in a relationship right now? I probably should have asked you that before I invited you for coffee tomorrow, huh?"

"Relax, Bentley. I'm not in a relationship. If you must know, I don't do relationships. If I don't set myself up for heartbreak and loss, then I never even have to worry about it."

"You're kidding, right? Surely, you've been in dozens of relationships and just haven't found Mister Right."

Shaking my head, "No, I'm not kidding. The last guy that I was in a relationship with was you."

"Me?" he questioned with skepticism in his voice. "That was almost two decades ago."

"I told you. I don't do relationships," I shrugged.

"I bet I can convince you otherwise," he said faintly, as thunder rolled in the distance.

The skies suddenly opened and a warm, summer rain began to fall on us.

"What did you say? I couldn't hear you over the thunder," I lied.

"It doesn't matter. You need to get home and into bed anyways. It's been a long night and morning will be here shortly. Make sure you take a few aspirin and drink a tall glass of water before putting yourself to bed," he said, taking off his coat and wrapping it around my bare shoulders.

"Maybe you should come over and tuck me in," I said, immediately wishing I could take back the words. It wasn't my intention to lead Bentley on. It was the wedding, the bouquet, the memories, the alcohol—yes, it was all those things—and nothing more, it couldn't be anything more. Who am I kidding? It's already a lot more. Even I can't deny the chemistry between us.

"Don't tempt me, Ireland. But, since I'm trying to behave myself, I'm going to put you in a taxi and I'm going to see you first thing in the morning."

My phone rang beside me. "Shit, I must have drifted back to sleep," I said to myself. I saw Bentley's name flash on the screen. How did he even get my number? He never even asked me for it.

"Hello," I answered, groggily.

"Ireland? Are you OK," he asked, frantically.

"Yeah, I'm fine. Why?"

"Because it's quarter after eight. You were supposed to be here fifteen minutes ago. Katie is freaking out."

"Crap! I woke up at seven, but my head was pounding. I just lay down for another minute and wanted to rest my eyes. I didn't plan on falling back asleep. Is she mad? Never mind, that's a stupid question. Of course she's mad. Fuck, she's going to kill me. Tell her I'll be there in twenty minutes. Oh my god, I look like hell." I rambled, as I heard Bentley laugh on the other end of the phone.

"Stop laughing at me! This is serious! And, come to think of it, how did you get my number anyways? You never asked me for it and I know Katie wouldn't dare give it to you without asking me first. Unless that was her way of punishing me for being late!"

"I'm sorry for laughing at you. I can just imagine that cute, little expression on your face—the same one you used to get when your mom would call you in for dinner. You'd scrunch your face all tight because you wanted to stay out all night and help me with the tree house."

"Seriously, I'm not ten anymore, Bentley," I said, looking in the mirror across from my bed and wincing when I saw the same expression on my face that he'd just described. How can he still know me so well after all these years?

"Trust me, I'm very well aware that you're not ten anymore, Ireland. My cock and I both noticed the grown woman that you've become."

I felt my heart skip a beat at his admission. "I'm hanging up now. I'll see you shortly, Bentley. And, don't think I'm letting you get away with you not telling me how you got my number."

"I'm counting on it, gorgeous. Drive safe and I'll see you soon," he said before disconnecting the line.

My body was betraying me. Bentley's husky voice mixed with the fresh scent of the cologne permeating off his coat that I'd brought to bed, had me wanting to pull my trusted vibrator out of the nightstand and pleasure myself. But, I didn't have another minute to spare. Instead, I ran into the bathroom, hoping I could get away with throwing my hair into a top-knot and spritzing on some perfume.

"Fuck me! My own reflection is going to haunt my dreams tonight," I mumbled to myself.

So much for my wishful thinking. I'd smudged my mascara during the night, leaving me with raccoon eyes and the snarled mess that was my hair was beyond the help of the standard messy bun. I'd even forgotten to remove the gardenia before I'd crawled into bed and that was now smooshed to the side of my head. I guess I was lucky I still wasn't in my dress.

Stripping off my pajamas, I hopped into the shower. The water had no chance to even get hot when I turned off the faucet and jumped back out. I looked at my reflection once again and although it wasn't perfect, it was definitely an improvement.

I towel dried my thick mane and grabbed an elastic band off the counter to quickly throw my hair up. I dusted on some light powder before running back into the bedroom where I hopped into my favorite pair of floral leggings and matched them with a light pink tunic. Slipping into a pair of ballet flats, I grabbed my purse and keys and exited my apartment. I quickly glanced at my phone and saw it was only twenty after eight. I did good for only five minutes.

Luckily my car was parked close to my apartment's main entrance and I didn't have to walk far. Just rushing to get ready had left me out of breath and thinking about heading back to the gym tomorrow morning. I slid behind the wheel of my cherry red Honda Accord and made the fifteen-minute drive to Greg's parents' house. I made sure to put on some mascara and lip gloss while I was stopped at the traffic lights. As I parked the car in the cul-de-sac, I quickly glanced in the rearview mirror to make sure I was presentable.

"Eh, not exactly the impression I want to give Bentley, but I guess it'll have to do," I muttered to myself, grabbing my purse and Bentley's jacket from the passenger seat.

Before I even had a chance to make it up the walkway, Katie had opened the front door and was standing on the front porch with hands on her hips.

"I'm sorry. I'm so sorry," I said, without even allowing her the chance to yell at me.

"Where the hell have you been? I was worried sick. I couldn't even enjoy my doughnut. And, you know how much I love doughnuts!" she yelled.

"Yeah, it really looks like I kept you from enjoying your

doughnut. The powdered sugar on your lips really tells a different story, though." I said, raising my eyebrows.

"Fine! You caught me, but in my defense, I hadn't had a doughnut in eight months! It still pisses me off that those little bastards are like twelve Weight Watchers points. Do you know how much it killed me not to eat doughnuts before the wedding? I never should've bought such a form-fitting dress. Take it from me, when you marry Bentley make sure you get a poofy dress," she said, licking the remaining powdered sugar from her lips.

"I think that powdered sugar has gone to your brain. Either that or Greg fucked you stupid last night," I said. "I'm not marrying anyone—let alone Bentley. Where would you get such an absurd idea?"

"From Bentley," she sassed.

"Wh—What do you mean from Bentley? I asked, wide-eyed.

"He told me about the bouquet. And about how he made you pick it up."

"That's it? That's all he told you?"

"Yes, that's all I needed to know."

"And, you got a marriage proposal out of all that? You know what, I love you, but I can't handle this nonsense today. Maybe I should just go home and we can talk when you get back from your honeymoon—when your head is back on straight." Maybe I was being rude, but Katie was seriously acting delusional. Just as I turned around and began to head back to my car, I felt his presence behind me once again. How was he able to do that?

"You're leaving before you even come in? What about our plans for coffee?" Bentley asked.

"She was just grabbing something from the car. Right, Ireland?" Katie said. Even she knew I would never leave her without a proper goodbye.

"Yeah, I actually left their wedding gift in my trunk," I answered.

"Oh, I'll come help you then," Bentley said, stepping out onto the front porch in his bare feet. I don't know how he did it, but even his feet were sexy. And, you know what they say about a man's feet . . .

After nearly four hours of watching Katie and Greg open about every kind of blender, toaster oven, mixer, countertop grill, and slow cooker imaginable, it was time to see them off. Seriously, who knew there were so many types of small kitchen appliances? As long as I had a microwave and Keurig, I was set for life.

After Katie and Greg loaded their luggage into the back of the taxi and we said our tearful goodbyes, they were off to Bora Bora for the next ten days.

"Are you going to be OK?" Bentley asked, rubbing circles on my back, as we watched the taxi back out of the driveway.

"Yes. I know I'm being ridiculous, but we haven't been apart for more than a day since we met. She's the only constant I've had in my life since . . ." I said, trailing off.

"You don't have to explain, Ireland. I wasn't making fun of you for being upset. I truly just want to make sure you're OK." I looked into his eyes and saw his sincerity.

"I really have missed you," I said, as I stood on my tiptoes to place a chaste kiss on his cheek. It was the first time I'd taken the initiative to kiss him. It may have only been on the cheek, but I hoped he could tell I was trying.

BENTLEY INSISTED ON driving to the coffeehouse and was I ever relieved when we drove up only to find a street filled with nothing but parallel parking. I'd never been able to master the skill myself, always trying to pull into the spot, but leaving the rear of my car crooked and sticking out in traffic. I didn't care to recount all the times I'd been honked at while struggling to park before finally giving up and driving off.

Bentley pulled up next to the car in front of the space and effortlessly backed into it as if the car were on autopilot. I laughed out loud without even saying a word.

"What's so funny?" he questioned, shifting into park and removing the keys from the ignition.

"You just made that look so simple."

"You've lost me. Made what look so simple? All I did was park a car," he shrugged.

"You didn't just PARK a car. You parallel parked a car. And, it only took you one shot!"

"Please tell me that you're kidding," he chuckled.

"No, I'm not kidding. You have skills."

"Those aren't the only skills I possess, Shamrock," he said with a wink.

"You're such a flirt," I sassed, slapping him on the shoulder.

"Kevin taught me how to parallel park before I was even

sixteen. He told me then that it would impress the ladies. I guess having an older brother does pay off. Remind me to thank him the next time I see him."

"I'll do that," I joked. "Seriously though—parallel parking has never been my forte."

"It's not that hard. I'll teach you sometime. In fact, I'll teach you all my skills."

"You're incorrigible."

"You love it," he said, before opening his door and sliding out, leaving me in the car alone.

"Probably more than I should," I mumbled to myself as Bentley came around and opened my door.

"Oh, such a gentleman," I said, stepping out of the Range Rover.

"Just call me Prince Charming," he said with a grin. Bentley's smile alone was enough to melt my panties right off. His teeth were perfectly straight and dazzling white.

I bowed my head, hoping he hadn't just caught me staring. "My breakfast is stuck in my teeth isn't it?" he asked, rubbing his front tooth.

I laughed, "No, quite the opposite actually. I can't get over how perfect they look."

"Oh, well Staci's father is an orthodontist. Her entire family takes great pride in oral hygiene," he said, rolling his eyes.

"Oh, I—I didn't realize."

"Shit, sorry, I probably shouldn't have brought up my ex-wife on our first date."

I took a deep breath before speaking. Did he really just call this a date? I didn't have time to worry about all the logistics right now. I just needed to focus on having a good time with Bentley over a cup of coffee. That should be simple enough, right?

Taking my silence as something more than it was, Bentley spoke, "I really am sorry, Shamrock. I won't bring her up again.

I promise. Way for me to kill the mood before we even step foot inside," he said, putting his hand on the small of my back, ushering me into the coffee shop.

"It's OK, Bentley. I want to get to know you again. She's been a major part of your life for so many years. You share a son. I would expect you to talk about her," I said, reassuringly.

Before opening the door, he stopped in front of the shop and pulled me into his chest. As if I'd been doing it my entire life, I instinctively leaned my head back on his chest.

"I love how easy this feels between us," Bentley whispered before placing a soft kiss on the top of my head. "I know eventually we'll have to talk about the hard stuff, but today I just want to keep it about us. Deal?"

"Deal," I promised before reaching for the door handle.

"Uh-uh," Bentley said, stopping me. "Prince Charming, remember?"

I gave Bentley my order before scoping out the coffeehouse to find us some seats. Being that it was a Sunday afternoon, the place was fairly empty minus a few summer school students feverishly typing on their laptops, presumably working on final papers before the upcoming holiday. We pretty much had our choice of seats, but it was the U-shaped booth lined with pillows nestled in the back corner that caught my eye. It was probably too cozy and intimate for two friends reconnecting, but I couldn't help but fall into the seat.

I'd scooted into the middle, propping my feet up beside me. Grabbing one of the pillows, I held it against my chest as Bentley came over with our beverages.

"It took me a minute to even find you over here," he said, sitting down in the booth. "Looks like you've already made yourself at home though," he added, pointing to my now bare feet.

"What? I like to be comfortable and I hate shoes and socks," I shrugged. "But, you already knew that because it's definitely not a new trait. Now hand over the caffeine," I said, taking one of the cups from his hands.

"Shit! That's hot!" I blurted out as some of the liquid sloshed over the side and onto my wrist.

"Serves you right for having grabby hands," Bentley said in mock disgust.

Putting my wrist to his lips, he cooed, "But, I suppose I can find it in my heart to kiss it and make it better."

In that moment, I felt my heart flutter inside my chest. How was it than in just twenty-four hours, Bentley had succeeded in weakening the impenetrable walls that I'd built around my heart?

"So, tell me about Jamie?" I interrupted, hoping to get my mind back on track.

He looked puzzled. "I thought you were refusing to call me that. You've only called me Bentley since we were reintroduced at the wedding."

"You'll always be Bentley, but I already know Bentley. I guess I want to get to know Jamie—even though I'll still call you Bentley," I laughed. "Did that make sense? Because it totally made sense in my head before I said it out loud."

"It made perfect sense. What do you want to know?"

"Everything. You played football for the University of Tennessee?" I asked, taking a sip from the cup sitting in front of me.

"Blech. What the hell is this shit?!? I yelled, spitting the liquid into my napkin.

"It's coffee, drama queen. I can already tell someone was a thespian in high school," Bentley said, rolling his eyes.

"Actually, yes, and in college too. I'll have you know that I played Alice in *Alice in Wonderland* and Dorothy in *The Wizard of Oz*. Now take your black coffee-shit and hand over my caramel-crème latte."

He swapped cups with me before answering, "I don't know how you drink that sweet shit. I feel like I'm wearing a sweater on my teeth."

"It's better than a cup of dirt like you're drinking!"

"I guess we'll just have to agree to disagree about this one. But, back to a more important issue."

"What's that?" I asked.

"Please tell me you still have those ruby slippers because I'd love nothing more than to see you sprawled out on my bed wearing nothing but those."

I felt my cheeks flush at his admission. "Is it—is it hot in here, or is it just—just me?" I stuttered.

"It's a little warm—yes, but you're the only thing in here that's hot. And, that's saying a lot since we're in a coffeehouse."

I couldn't contain my laughter. "Well you did have me turned on until you said that. You're so fucking cheesy."

"At least I can still make you laugh," he said with a smirk. Even under his day-old scruff, I still saw the same dimpled cheeks that I'd fallen in love with as a kid.

It wasn't until the barista had refilled our drinks about ten times that I took a look at my phone to check the time. I was shocked when I saw that it was already nearly seven o'clock. We'd spent the afternoon reminiscing and catching up on our lives over the last two decades. I'd heard everything from Bentley's time at the University of Tennessee playing football to earning his degree in architectural engineering.

Although Bentley said he wanted to keep the conversation just about us, the topic of Staci did come up again. The two had met as undergrads and after a year of dating Staci became pregnant with Tanner during their last year of college. Bentley graduated at the top of his class, but Staci didn't finish and followed Bentley to Detroit where he'd obtained a job at a prominent architectural firm. The two got married and moved their small family from Tennessee to Michigan.

That's where he met Greg and the two hit it off right away. After just three years, they both left the firm and made the decision to become partners in their own firm. I could only feel impressed with everything he'd been able to accomplish and overcome at such a young age.

I could tell he didn't want to get into their actual marriage, or the way things ended between the two of them. I suppose if we were to continue doing whatever it was we were doing then that would be a topic for another day.

He talked about Tanner and how his son wanted to follow in his dad's footsteps and takeover the architectural firm someday. I could see the joy in Bentley's eyes each time he told me a story about Tanner and could tell his son meant the world to him. I knew instantly that if he was anything like his father then he was a good kid.

I went on to tell him about my job as a counselor, working primarily with orphaned children. It had always been my desire to turn my negative experience into something positive and I never wanted children to feel alone and scared. I didn't want them to blame themselves as if they'd ever done anything wrong. Although I was still living with my own fears and insecurities, I hoped I was making a positive impact on their lives.

As more time passed, I found myself cuddling closer into Bentley's side. He had his arm propped up on the cushion behind me and I felt safer here than I had in years. It was like no time had passed between us.

"Hey, I have a crazy idea," Bentley said, sipping his coffee. I still couldn't believe he was drinking that shit black.

"Yes, you should try the flavored creamer," I responded with a playful wink.

"You're cute when you're trying to be sassy, but that wasn't my idea."

"No? Well at least you still think I'm cute after a night of drinking and a five-minute shower. But, if hazelnut cappuccino isn't in the plans then let's hear your crazy idea."

"You know what, never mind. It's really too crazy," he said, shaking his head.

"Would you seriously just tell me!"

"Nope," he answered, making sure to pop the "p."

"Fine, I suppose it's time for me to get going anyways," I said, placing my feet on the floor and sliding over in the booth.

"Wait. Always did know how to get what you wanted, didn't you?"

"Maybe," I paused, waiting for him to spill it. "So, are you actually going to tell me this crazy idea of yours, or do I need a lid to take this latte to go?" I said, pointing at my Styrofoam cup.

"My mom's having knee replacement surgery on Monday and I'm leaving for Tennessee this weekend—just for a few days. I know it's probably too soon, but I was wondering if you'd like to go with me. I thought maybe instead of getting a hotel, we could stay at the cabin."

My eyes widened and I put my hand to my mouth. Bentley was right. This was definitely too soon. This was certainly a crazy idea. But, why if it was so crazy, did I actually want to go?

"Never mind. I told you it was insane. Just forget I even asked. Time to change the subject—tell me more about your job," Bentley rambled.

"Yes," I said, even surprising myself.

"Yes? Yes, you'll go with me?"

There was nothing but pure excitement radiating from his eyes. I couldn't change my mind now. I was all in. Just twenty-four hours ago, Bentley was still only a part of my past, but now all I wanted was a future with him. In just twenty-four short hours, this man had destroyed everything I'd ever believed about love and relationships.

I blew out a breath of air and rested my head back to look up at the ceiling. I'd forgotten I wasn't alone until I heard Bentley ask me once again, "Ireland, are you OK? Did you really just say that you'd go with me? Or, am I imagining things?"

I raised my head and looked into his deep brown eyes once

again, "No, you aren't imagining things. I will go with you. What about Tanner? Will he be going with us?"

I don't know why that idea petrified me even more. If I wanted to be a part of Bentley's life then I would need to be a part of Tanner's life, too. I dealt with teenagers on a daily basis at work, and got along well with many of them, but Tanner was different. His opinions of me would have an effect on my future—my future with Bentley. Of course I wanted to spend time with Tanner and get to know him, I just wasn't sure if I was ready to do it quite so soon. After all, I was still just getting reacquainted with his father.

"No, school is out for a few more weeks and he wants to stay here with his friends. He'll be staying here with Staci. I do hope you can meet him soon though."

I gave him a weak smile, hoping he wouldn't sense my fear. "I'd like that."

Sensing my apprehension, Bentley leaned into me and grabbed my hand in his. Our eyes locked and he whispered, "Don't worry, Shamrock. He'll love you, you'll see. After all, you aren't very difficult to love."

I was relieved when an incoming text on my phone took me away from our conversation. I didn't really want to delve any further into what Bentley was telling me right now.

> *Katie: We just landed in Los Angeles. We're here for two hours and then we're off to Tahiti. With any luck we'll get to Bora Bora before we're both eighty. Why didn't you tell me this flight would suck donkey balls? P.S. How'd it go with Jamie, or is it Bentley? And, did he Sham-ROCK your world?!?!?!*

I chuckled at Katie's way with words.

> *Ireland: OK! Safe travels! We'll talk next week! Love your face!*

I was hoping she would take my curt response as a sign that I was still busy with Bentley and would let it go. My phone vibrated on the table once more. *Wishful thinking.*

> *Katie: OK, I knew I was going to have to pry it out of you, but I thought you would give me a little more of a tease than that . . . Wait a minute! Are you still with him?!?!?!*

> *Ireland: I am not! Now go and enjoy your honeymoon!*

> *Katie: You so are! You know you're a terrible liar! I can tell you're lying to me over text!*

There was really no use arguing with her. Just when I was about to reply, I saw Bentley's phone light up on the table.

"Let me guess—it's Greg," I said.

"Actually, I think it's Katie using Greg's phone. It's not like Greg to ask me how my date went," he laughed.

"She's never going to hear the end of this from me," I sighed.

"Maybe I should get you home so you can call her before she drives you crazy."

"Sadly I think you're right," I said, scooting out of the booth.

"I'M GOING TO be busy the next few days finishing up a project, but will you have dinner with me on Wednesday," Bentley asked, as we pulled up next to my car. "We can talk more about next weekend then."

"Dinner sounds good, but let me cook you something at my place."

"Are you sure? I'd be happy to take you out."

"I know, but I figured we'd have more privacy at my place and I'd love to cook for you. Hard to believe, but I'm actually pretty good at it. I took a few culinary classes as extracurricular back in college. Greg and Katie can't cook to save their lives, so

I figured someone needed to learn. And, please, don't tell her I told you that," I chuckled.

"Your secret is safe with me. Truth-be-told, I always suspected that was the case since I've worked with the guy for over ten years and I've never once been invited to dinner at their place. But, dinner at your place sounds perfect. I'll text you tomorrow and we'll figure out the details," he said, leaning over to peck me on the nose

Although the sun was already beginning to set, I didn't want my time with Bentley to end. I couldn't believe I'd spent the entire day with him. It felt so natural—so easy. Like we'd spent every day together for the past eighteen years.

As if reading my mind, Bentley leaned into me once again. "I've missed you, Ireland."

I didn't have time to respond before Bentley captured my lips with his. He didn't start slowly like he had yesterday on the dance floor. Today his lips were punishing mine, and I was enjoying every minute of it. He consumed me. It was raw—carnal even. After what seemed like several minutes, we both pulled away gasping for air. I wasn't sure if the stars I saw were from the kiss, or from lack of oxygen to the brain. It took everything I had not to strip naked in the front seat and let him violate me in his car.

As if he could sense my desires, "You need to get into your car and leave before I throw you into the backseat. And, I'd rather our first time not be a quickie in my Rover."

I blushed—either from his ability to read my mind, or from his mention of our first time. Instead of speaking, I put my hand on the door, struggling to find the handle.

"I don't know how you do it, but you're cute when you're flustered," Bentley said, pulling me back to steal one more kiss. This one was sweeter, but still left me heated and aching for more.

"I'll see you on Wednesday?" I asked, stepping out of the

SUV.

"You better believe you will. I'll text you tomorrow with a time. Drive safe, Shamrock."

I shut the door and slid into my car hoping that Bentley would drive off. No such luck. He certainly was a perfect gentleman and had no intention of leaving me there alone. I put my keys in the ignition and waved at Bentley before driving off. Luckily he didn't follow me home and I was able to pull over about a block away in order to gather my thoughts.

I put my car in park as I banged my head against the steering wheel, wondering what the hell I'd gotten myself into. Were we dating? Bentley had called it a date earlier. I don't date. Do I want to date? Are we just friends? Am I OK with being just friends? My mind was swarming with questions until fists knocking on my window scared me senseless. Looking up, I saw two young boys staring back at me. I started my engine and rolled my window down a bit.

"Miss are you OK? Your horn has been blasting for five minutes. We were over a block playing street hockey and we decided to come and investigate. We saw you slumped over and were afraid you'd passed out."

So lost in my own thoughts, I hadn't even heard my horn. I hoped the people whose house I'd stopped in front of were out for the evening, or they had probably already called the police on me.

"I'm fine. Must have just fallen asleep for a minute," I lied. "Just a long day. Thank you for checking on me, boys."

They nodded and were on their way. I, too, decided to head for home where I would, hopefully, work this all out before I was supposed to see Bentley again.

Chapter Six

ARRIVING FOR WORK on Monday morning, I was surprised to see a dozen red roses on my desk. Assuming they were from Katie and Greg, probably thanking me for my help over the weekend, I was even more stunned when I saw they were actually from Bentley.

> Shamrock,
>
> I'm so glad life brought us back together this weekend. It was great catching up with you yesterday. I can't wait to see your beautiful face on Wednesday.
>
> Love,
>
> The Hopeless Romantic

He really wasn't taking the standard "seventy-two hour" rule very seriously. He'd even texted me shortly after I'd returned home from our coffee date to make sure I'd arrived safely. I sat with my phone in hand for several seconds before typing out a response—deleting it—and retyping another.

That process went on for about five minutes before I finally settled on telling him that I'd indeed made it home safely, was heading to bed and would talk to him in the next few days. I was actually a little surprised—and maybe even a little disappointed—that I hadn't heard from him again. I should've known he wasn't going to let it go that easily.

Since I'd gotten little sleep the night of the wedding, I decided on going to bed early, but for the second night in a row, I tossed and turned with images of Bentley floating in my dreams. It was nearly impossible to drag myself out of bed this morning, but I knew I had two new cases coming in today and couldn't just pass off my responsibilities on my co-workers because my head was in the clouds over Bentley. Seriously, I was starting to sound like some love-struck teenager.

Just as I was typing out a text message to thank Bentley for the flowers, Susan, my boss at the center, walked into my office.

"Good morning, Ireland. Just so you know, on top of the two cases we were already expecting, we have teenage twins—both girls—coming in as well. Their mom and dad were both killed in a traffic accident over the weekend and they don't have any immediate family. We'll have to work quickly to place them with a foster family. It'd be best if we didn't have to separate them."

Her words took me back to the crash that had taken everyone I'd ever loved. Bentley may not have died with them that day, but he'd been taken away just the same. The thought of losing him all over again was too much to bear. In that moment, I felt myself beginning to patch that wall around my heart that Bentley had manage to crack in just a few short days.

"Yeah, of course, I'll get right on that," I said. "Are the girls here yet? I'd like to speak with them as soon as possible."

"No, they should be here in about thirty minutes. I'll make sure to send them right down once we get them checked in," Susan answered. As she began to turn back towards the door, her eyes landed on the vase of flowers on my desk. "Oh, those are beautiful! I didn't realize you were seeing anyone," she said with a smile.

"Oh, thank you. And, I'm not. I'm not seeing anyone," I added, clarifying. I didn't need any office gossip. I'd managed to keep my personal life, or lack thereof, pretty private in the five years that I'd worked there and I intended to keep it that way. In fact, I didn't think many of my co-workers, aside from Susan who asked during the interview process, even knew my story, or my motivation for becoming a social worker for orphaned children.

"Well, whoever sent them must think you're pretty special, Ireland. Because they're gorgeous. And, if I must say, I thought you seemed more chipper this morning," she said, smiling.

Her words caught me off guard. Not really knowing how to respond to her revelation, I was relieved when my phone vibrated in my hand giving me a quick out. I looked down to see an incoming text from Bentley. I'd gotten so caught up in my conversation with Susan that I'd forgotten about my unfinished text thanking him for the flowers.

"That must be the mystery man. I can tell because that smile of yours actually reached your eyes. I'm not sure I've ever actually seen that before. Make sure you keep him around," she said, turning to leave my office.

I had to give her credit. She was really saying all the right things. It was definitely from all those years working with the children in the foster system. It may have worked on me twenty years ago, but I'd spent the last decade using those same lines on children. Sure, I wanted to believe the words I told them—for their own sake, but sadly my heart knew the tragic truth.

The hurt was too deep—for me at least. Somehow, though, I'd managed to tell hundreds of orphaned children through the years that it would be OK when I myself have never truly been OK. I always hoped for them it would be different, and maybe I would actually help play a part in their road to recovery. I would tell them that their lives are worth living.

I needed to take my own advice and start living my life the same way I'd dreamed of all those years ago, but I couldn't properly do that if I was still constantly in fear of loss.

And, if I was being honest with myself, Susan was right about something. I was happier this weekend—smiling more than I had most of my life. Maybe it was Katie, maybe it was the wedding, or maybe it was my reunion with Bentley.

I sighed knowing that it was probably Bentley. This weekend was the first time in nearly twenty years that I'd actually felt like everything in my life was truly going to be OK. I needed to take this leap of faith. I needed to open my heart and trust that Bentley wouldn't leave me. And with that revelation, the wall completely fell. I just wasn't sure I was ready to tell Bentley yet—maybe I'd get the courage to tell him over dinner later this week.

My phone vibrated again with Bentley's incoming text.

> *Bentley: I thought I would've heard from you by now. I hope the flowers didn't get sent to the wrong office because if they did then some lucky lady is going to think we have a date on Wednesday. Either that or you have another Hopeless Romantic in your life and you thanked him. In which case, who is he so I can go slash his tires?*

Laughing at his message, I began to type out my response.

> *Ireland: I'm so sorry! I was typing out a message when my boss came in to tell me about a new case we have today. I got caught up in our conversation and I completely forgot what I was doing. The flowers are beautiful, though. Thank you!*

> *Ireland: P.S. You're definitely the only Hopeless Romantic in my life. No need to go crazy and slash any tires!! ;)*

Bentley: You don't have to apologize. I figured you were just busy. I'm just giving you a hard time. The flowers aren't nearly as beautiful as you are, but I'm glad you liked them. I'll let you get back to work. I know how Mondays can be. I should probably start looking over some client files myself. I'll talk to you soon, Shamrock.

Ireland: OK. Thanks again! TTYL.

THE ORPHANED TWINS, Christy and Sierra, had come into my office alone and scared. They confided in me that their worst fear was now that they'd lost both their mom and dad that they were going to lose each other, too. I assured them that I would do everything in my power to make sure that wouldn't be the case. I knew how much they needed each other, and knew how much that loss on top of the loss of their parents would affect them for their entire lives. I'd even considered taking them home with me, but knew my small two-bedroom condo wasn't the place for two teenage girls.

Working tirelessly for three straight days, I tried to place these girls with a suitable foster family. Fortunately, at around noon, I was finally able to arrange the perfect environment for the two. I'd found a middle-aged couple who'd already raised a grown son who was willing to take in the girls—together. It was the perfect scenario.

I'd completed the last of the paperwork for the girls' transfer and was getting ready to head out of the office early for once. I wanted time to stop at the grocery store to pick up a few items for the meal I'd planned, as well as get home in time to tidy up and throw a load of laundry in the wash before Bentley arrived around six o'clock.

For the last two nights, he'd called me as soon as we got out of work and we talked until it was time for bed. I wasn't sure how we'd managed to keep the conversation going for hours each night, but there was never any awkward silence between us. Well maybe except for that brief period when I'd fallen asleep while talking to him the night before. I couldn't help it. The lack of sleep from Bentley running marathons in my head each night was finally catching up to me. He'd made sure to call me out for my subtle snoring though. I was so embarrassed and tried to blame it on bad reception, but he wasn't falling for it.

I was actually looking forward to having Bentley over to my place for dinner. It may be hard to believe, but in my thirty-two years, I'd never cooked for a man before. Actually, I'd never even let one inside my home. Well except for Greg, but he didn't count. Oh, and Steve my handyman, but I suppose he didn't really count either.

Nope, after a one-night stand, I'd rather be the one leaving his place in the morning—doing the walk of shame—than having to be faced with the uncomfortable situation of him wanting to stay for breakfast, or even worse—wanting to spend the entire day with me. "Dump and Dash." That had always been my motto—up until five days ago when Bentley had managed to turn my entire world upside down.

Leaving Susan with my files on the twins, I was headed toward the elevator when my phone pinged with an incoming text. Looking down, I smiled when I saw Bentley's name light up the screen.

> *Bentley: Hey Shamrock, I hate to do this, but I need to cancel our plans for tonight. Tanner got into a fight with some neighborhood kids today, and I don't think I should leave him alone tonight. I think he's having a more difficult time with the divorce than he's letting on. Anyway, I'm really sorry, but I just think I should stay with him tonight. We're still on for this weekend though, right?*

Although I was disappointed, I completely understood that Bentley's first priority had to be his son.

Ireland: I'd be lying if I said I wasn't looking forward to seeing you tonight, but Tanner needs to come first. I can make you dinner some other time. And, yes, we're still on for this weekend. What are the two of you going to do tonight?

Bentley: Well, I thought I would put my culinary expertise to use and pour us both a big bowl of Captain Crunch and then we'll probably watch a movie. Super exciting right?

Ireland: Sounds like a blast! LOL

Bentley: It's not the excitement I was planning on tonight that's for sure. ;)

Ireland: James Bentley Roberts . . . Are you flirting with me over text message?

Bentley: Maybe. Perhaps yes. OK, yes. I hope that's OK.

Ireland: This might sound crazy, but what if you both came over for dinner. I bought plenty of food and I have this new game that I bought for the kids who I counsel. I mean unless you were really looking forward to that Captain Crunch and in which case just forget about the whole thing.

I hit send before I could delete everything I'd just typed. What had gotten into me? Was I really ready to meet Bentley's son? And, I totally lied to him because I hadn't even purchased any food yet! What the hell had gotten into me?

What felt like several minutes ticked by without a response from Bentley. I was typing out a message telling him it was a mistake when my phone buzzed in my hand. Staring at Bentley's name for a few seconds, I opened the message. I'm not sure why I was scared of his response. What if he didn't want me to meet his son?

> *Bentley: Seriously? You're sure you have enough food for both of us? You know we're both growing boys, right? Unfortunately, one of us is only growing out anymore though.*

> *Ireland: Yes, I'm sure. I have plenty here. And, trust me, I'm pretty sure I could see your abs under your T-shirt on Sunday. You're definitely not growing out.*

I slapped myself on the forehead after hitting send. Shit! What's wrong with me? Did I just admit to him that I was checking him out? I mean it was hard not to—the way his white Tee clung to his sculpted chest and biceps. I found myself resisting the urge to lift it up to take a look at the six-pack that I knew lay underneath.

> *Bentley: I knew you were checking me out!*

> *Ireland: Caught me. Now are you coming, or not? I have dinner to prepare.*

> *Bentley: Yes, we'll both be there. And, Shamrock . . .*

> *Ireland: Yeah?*

> *Bentley: Something is most definitely growing out. It just may not be my gut that I'm referring to.*

Holy hell. My face blushed as I stared down at my phone screen. I didn't even know how to respond to him. A gentleman's voice alerted me to the present.

"Excuse me, miss? Were you waiting to go down? It's been

open for several seconds, but you didn't appear to be moving," he said with a chuckle. "I didn't want to be rude and step in front of you."

I'd been so wrapped up in my text conversation and now Bentley's not so subtle flirting that I'd forgotten I was waiting for an elevator.

"Oh, yes, sorry. Thank you," I said, joining him in the elevator. I quickly typed out a response to Bentley. I kept it brief, hoping he wouldn't notice.

Ireland: I'll see you both at six then.

Bentley: See you at six. And, don't think I'm letting this go that easily.

Crap, he noticed . . .

Chapter Seven

I'D JUST PULLED my four-cheese, baked ziti from the oven and was wiping the splatter from my homemade pasta sauce from the kitchen counter when there came a knock at the front door. Suddenly my palms began to sweat and butterflies took nervous flight in my belly. Was I really doing this? Was I ready to meet Bentley's son? What if I didn't know what to say to him? What if he hated me?

Again there was a knock at the door. *Shit!* I took a deep breath, threw my rag in the sink and wiped the back of my hands against the denim shorts I'd thrown on after work.

Opening the door, my eyes immediately raked Bentley up and down. He was wearing a pair of khaki golf shorts and a black polo shirt. I couldn't help but notice the strain on the shirt's sleeves from his bulging biceps. I so badly wanted to ask him to turn around so I could check out his backside.

Bentley cleared his throat and it was then that I noticed Tanner standing next to his father. Other than his blond hair, he was a spitting image of the Bentley I remembered from decades ago.

"Hi! You must be Tanner," I said, offering my hand after they'd both entered the foyer.

"Wow! You're a quick one," he said, rolling his eyes at me.

Dropping my hand, I looked up at Bentley, stunned by his

son's immediate attitude. *This was going to be a long night.*

"Tanner! We talked about this in the car. Ireland was being polite and said hello. Do you have something to say in return," he said sternly.

"Fine! Hi, Ireland."

"Hi," I said, hesitantly. "It's nice to meet you."

"Uh huh," he mumbled.

Bentley jumped in, trying to save me, or maybe himself, from this awkward situation.

"Dinner smells delicious. We both came extra hungry. Didn't we, champ?" he said, patting Tanner on the back.

"I'm not really that hungry. Mom fed me a few hotdogs before she dropped me off at your house."

"Humor me, son," Bentley said gruffly, leading Tanner to the dining room table where I'd already set out dishes and silverware.

Tanner was quiet throughout most of dinner. I should've been better at this. I talked to children on a daily basis. I had to keep it in perspective that this was all new to him. He probably wanted his mom and dad together. I mean what kid doesn't want that? He knew they weren't married anymore, but he probably still held out hope—and now here I was—probably destroying what little hope he had for their reconciliation.

Our conversation had become a tennis match of back and forth questions—me asking them and his one word responses.

"What's your favorite subject?" I asked.

"Gym."

"Do you play any sports?"

"Yes."

"What's your favorite?"

"Football."

I sighed. Seriously, how did news people make it look so easy? They knew exactly how to phrase a question and get more than a one-word answer.

Sensing my frustration, Bentley looked over and gave me a sympathetic look. This relationship was going to end before it ever had a chance to really begin. Bentley wouldn't want anything to do with me after seeing how much his son loathed me.

"Hey Tanner, I think I see an Xbox One sitting over there by the TV. Why don't you ask Ireland what games she has? Maybe you can play something while we clean up the kitchen?" Bentley said.

"Nah, she probably only has crap girly games. I'm ready to get out of here. Can we just go home—please?"

"Tanner James Roberts! You're being rude to my friend. Now apologize!"

"I don't want to apologize. I just want to go home. I'll just call Mom to come and get me."

I knew I should probably leave and let Bentley and Tanner finish their conversation in private, but I found myself frozen in place.

"Sorry," Bentley mouthed in my direction before turning his attention back to his son. "You're not involving your mother. You're lucky I didn't force you to stay in your room for the entire night."

"I'm lucky? I'm only not in my room because you wanted to drag me over here so you could kiss your girlfriend. This doesn't have anything to do with me!"

My cheeks flushed and my jaw dropped.

"That's enough, young man!" Bentley said, sternly. "First you'll apologize to Ireland and then we're leaving. You're grounded for an entire month!"

"A month?!?! But I was supposed to go to the Lions' preseason game with Jeremy in two weeks. Please, Dad. I'm sorry. I take it back."

"Too little, too late," Bentley said, his jaw ticking.

"But, Dad, please! I'm sorry, Ireland!" he shouted, tears streaming down his cheeks.

"Bentley," I said, barely above a whisper. "I—I accept his apology. I think you should reconsider and let him go to the football game."

"You do?" Tanner questioned, surprise evident in his voice.

"Yeah, I do. And, I forgive you. Actually, I'd like it if you'd both reconsider and stay a bit longer. If you don't like my video game selection, then maybe we can find a movie?"

"I guess we could watch a movie. If it's OK with my dad," Tanner said, hesitantly. I could already tell that his hard exterior was softening. "What do you say, Dad?"

"I think we still need to go home, Son. We have a lot to discuss," Bentley said, his anger subsiding.

I gave Bentley a pleading look. I knew this was about punishing Tanner, but I really needed a chance to make this work with his son. "I really wish you would reconsider. I even have a Boston cream pie in the fridge. I was going on the assumption that it was still your favorite. I hope I'm right."

"Well, I have a hard enough time telling him no. I'm definitely screwed if I have to tell you both no. And, you throw in Boston cream pie, which is still my favorite, by the way, and I'm a dead man walking."

"Looks like you're staying then. Let me go slice that pie." I said, clearing the table of the dinner dishes. "Tanner, why don't you pick out a movie."

"Would it be OK if I actually look at your video games first? I really wish I would've brought my Madden game over. I honestly never expected you to have such a cool video game system."

"Oh, I actually have the new Madden game," I said nonchalantly.

"You do?" they both said in unison.

"It just came out a week ago," Tanner added, shock evident in his voice.

"Uh yeah. You might actually be surprised by what you find over there. I'm kind of a video game nerd."

Bentley helped me carry the rest of the dishes to the kitchen as Tanner started rummaging through my games.

"I have to admit, I didn't see you as much of a video game enthusiast either," Bentley said, as I ran some hot water to soak the dishes.

"Really? We always played them as kids? Why did you think I wouldn't still?"

"I figured you only played them to humor me. I was always under the impression that you never really cared too much for them."

I paused for a moment and bit down on my lip before responding. His question seemed simple enough, but my emotions were raw.

"You're right. I did only play them because you liked them, but then when you weren't there anymore they still brought me comfort. When I played them I would think about all the times we were together and all the memories we shared. I saved my allowance money and bought every game thinking you'd probably bought it too and I would pretend we were still playing them together," I rambled, keeping my eyes locked on the floor. "I know it probably sounds stupid."

"Ireland, look at me," Bentley said, placing three fingers on my chin. "It doesn't sound stupid at all. In fact, since we're being so honest, I'm kind of turned on by it," he added, wiggling his eyebrows.

I smirked and swatted him in the chest. "You really are crazy."

"Crazy about you," he said, placing a gentle kiss on my forehead. We hadn't even shared a real kiss tonight, but my body was buzzing for him. How he was able to do it with such a simple gesture, I'll never know, but I wanted him to take me right there on the kitchen island.

"Wow! You really do have some awesome games, Ireland. I don't know what to choose," Tanner yelled from the living room. I pulled away from Bentley, remembering that only a wall separated us from his son.

"We should probably get the pie ready," I said, grabbing the tin and the Reddi-Wip can from the refrigerator. Before I had a chance to spray the whipped topping onto the pie, Bentley grabbed the aerosol can from my hands. He shook it and sprayed a huge dollop into his mouth.

"I can't believe you just did that!" I exclaimed.

"Why not? We used to do it all the time as kids! You don't remember?" he mumbled, spraying whipped cream as he spoke.

"Of course, I remember!" I chuckled, yanking the can from his grasp and spraying my own mouth.

"I forgot how good this stuff tasted," I laughed, swallowing the airy confection.

Bentley came over and licked the corner of my mouth. "Sorry, you had a little whipped cream on your lips. I couldn't let it go to waste."

"I wish I'd left more," I whimpered.

"I wish I could just have you for dessert. Why don't you pack a can of this for the weekend," Bentley whispered in my ear. "We won't have any distractions—nothing to come between us. Just you and me."

His promise left me speechless. I just stood there looking up at him like a deer caught in headlights. It wasn't until we heard Tanner telling us that he'd decided on Madden that I remembered we were still standing in my kitchen and that I had a pie to serve.

"Ready for me to kick your ass?" Bentley asked, grabbing the entire pie and one fork.

"Whatever! And, you need to share that pie," I screamed, running out of the kitchen behind him.

"TOUCHDOWN!" TANNER SCREAMED. "Dad, Ireland is

totally kicking your butt. That's her fourth TD."

"Thanks, Son. I can see the score. I didn't really need the reminder," Bentley chuckled.

"Interception!" I yelled, jumping off the couch.

"Are you letting her win, Dad?"

"Obviously!" Bentley said, as my guy ran the ball into the end zone to score my fifth touchdown of the game.

"You wish, Roberts!" I said, as I stood and shook my bootie around the living room.

Bentley laughed, "What are you doing? Get back here so I can make my epic comeback."

"I'm doing my victory dance!" I said, blocking his view of the screen.

"Well, now you just aren't playing fair," he said, pulling me down on his lap as the game clock expired.

"Why don't you show me your touchdown dance? Oh wait, you would've had to score a touchdown first," I said with a smirk. "After all, I thought you were going to show me how it was done."

"You're asking for it, Shamrock. I'm rusty that's all. I haven't played this game in months. I'll get you next time," Bentley insisted.

"Dad, what are you talking about? We just played this last night," Tanner piped up.

"Busted!" I screamed as Bentley started tickling my sides and pulled me in for a quick kiss. Somehow this really had turned into a perfect night. Bentley held me on the couch for a few more minutes while Tanner was distracted by the game stats.

"Unbelievable. She had over five hundred passing yards!" Tanner mumbled to himself. "Ireland, are you ready to face me now?"

Bentley gave me another chaste kiss on the cheek and looked down toward his watch. "Tanner, I think we better get going. I have to work tomorrow and your mother will be at the house early to pick you up for the weekend. Maybe we can come back next week sometime and you can face Ireland," Bentley said, sounding hopeful.

"Please, Dad. Just one more game."

"I can take him down quick. Just like you taught me all those years ago," I whispered in Bentley's ear so only he would hear.

He gave me a knowing smirk. "OK, but just one more and then we're heading home."

Just as promised, it was only a matter of minutes before I had Tanner begging me for mercy.

"Ireland, how did you get so good?" Tanner asked. "I really thought my dad was letting you win, but I see now that he wasn't."

"I had a good teacher," I said, glancing over at Bentley. "Your dad and I used to play this when we were kids. He was the one who got me interested in gaming. The day I met him he actually was playing Gameboy."

"Gameboy?" Tanner asked. "What the heck is that?"

"Wow, kid. Way to make your old man feel—old."

"But, Dad, you are old."

Bentley and I started laughing uncontrollably on the couch and before we knew it, Tanner had started in. The sound was music to my ears. Maybe this would actually work out after all.

When we all had time to catch our breaths, Bentley announced that it was time for the two of them to leave. We all sat up and headed to the door. "I'll see you on Friday," Bentley said, pulling me against his body and placing a soft kiss on my lips. I didn't want to pull away from him, but I knew Tanner was watching us.

"I'm looking forward to it," I said, giving him another quick peck on the lips.

"It was nice meeting you, Tanner," I said.

"You too, Ireland," he said, placing his arms around my neck for a quick hug. "I actually had a really good time tonight. I hope we can have a rematch soon."

I wasn't expecting Tanner to hug me, but I was glad he had.

"You're welcome here anytime, Tanner," I said, as he walked out onto the porch giving Bentley and me a moment to ourselves.

"I'll talk to you tomorrow. And, if I didn't tell you earlier, good game," he said, spinning me around and slapping my ass like I was one of the guys in the locker room after a high school football game.

I just smiled and stood on my tip toes to give Bentley a chaste kiss. He deepened it briefly before pulling away.

"If I don't stop now, I won't be able to walk out that door. Just know, I'm not stopping this weekend," he whispered, before turning to leave.

I closed the door behind them and sank to the floor in relief. Tanner had been able to steal another piece of my heart right along with his father. I rested my head against the back of the door and said a silent prayer that I would recover if I ever lost them.

Chapter Eight

BENTLEY WAS COMING to pick me up in just a few short hours and I still hadn't packed a thing. I sat on the floor of my walk-in closet with a pile of clothes strewn about. I was only going for a few days, but I felt like I needed to pack for an entire month. It was the middle of summer, but we were going to the mountains. I could be in shorts and a bikini top during the day, but would need a hoodie at night. And, I didn't know what Bentley had planned for the evenings. I knew he'd want to spend some time with his mom during the day, but knowing him he'd made reservations for dinner at some fancy restaurants—which would require at least one little black dress, and jewelry to accessorize. And, shoes—footwear was an entirely different predicament all together. *Where is Katie when I need her.* I sighed in frustration as my phone jingled beside me.

"Seriously, how did you know I needed you right now?" I said, without even properly greeting my best friend.

"Instinct," she laughed. "I knew you were leaving with Bentley in a few hours and I figured you were going crazy. I take it by your 'hello,' or lack thereof that I'm correct?"

"I don't know what to pack!" I yelled in desperation through the phone. "Seriously, I wish there were like some sort of time travel portal that could get you from Bora Bora to my bedroom with a snap of my fingers."

"Sorry, no such luck," she said.

"We really need to get on that then. Think of all the millions we could make."

"OK, well you contact the investors on that *Shark Tank* show and tell me when to show up."

"I'll get right on that, but in the meantime, I need some serious help. What the hell am I supposed to pack?" I said, frantically.

"I'm still not following. Does it really matter? Won't you be walking around 'nekked,' and getting busy on a bearskin rug the entire time?"

"There's not a bearskin rug, asshole."

"Caught ya! You didn't deny walking around in your birthday suit, or getting busy! Oh, and there's totally a bearskin rug," Katie chuckled.

"Whatever. I will not confirm, or deny anything. And, how the fuck would you know if there's a bearskin rug?" I said, wiping the tears from my eyes from uncontrollable laughter.

"Greg told me about it. He went down there on some boys' fishing weekend a few years ago. He says it's the cheesiest thing ever, but he secretly wants to get one for the bedroom. He won't admit it, but I know he wants one. It's right up there with a mirror for the ceiling."

"Eww, seriously! I've heard enough. I don't need to know about your weird sexcapades. Besides, you need to tell me what to pack already. Bentley is going to be here in less than two hours and I still need to shower."

"Don't forget to shave—everywhere," she interjected.

"I'm ignoring you." I said, scrunching my face with the realization that I did in fact need some maintenance down there.

"You do know that if you were really ignoring me, you wouldn't have first told me you were ignoring me."

"Ugh! Would you stop being a smartass and help me pack. Why do I get the feeling that you're drunk anyways?"

"I'm not drunk. Well, unless you count the three mimosas

I've had at every meal since I've been here," she said, hiccupping.

"Oh my god. You're ridiculous. I'm hanging up and Facetiming you so you can see my closet. You're helping me even if you're plastered."

"I'm not pla–." I ended the call before she'd even finished denying her current inebriated status. I quickly dialed her again using the Facetime feature on my iPhone. "stered," she finished as she answered the call.

After about thirty minutes, I'd finally packed three suitcases. It was probably way too much, but Katie really wasn't much help and I ended up packing everything around me—I figured I'd rather have too much than too little."

"SERIOUSLY, FOUR SUITCASES?" Bentley asked with a raised brow.

"No, I only have three, thank you very much."

"One, two, three, four. There are definitely four bags there, Shamrock. I think you need to watch the counting episode of Sesame Street again. You know the one with the stuffed Muppet, Dracula guy."

"The Count?" I deadpanned, not amused by his attempt at humor.

"Yes, that's it. I guess that would've been the obvious name choice," he laughed. "Do you want me to check the showtimes on Public Broadcasting," he asked, grabbing his phone out of his pocket.

"Really? Are you done? Because the fourth bag you pointed at isn't a suitcase—it's my purse."

"Well when your purse is big enough to hold everything and the kitchen sink then I count it as a suitcase."

"Why do I continuously allow myself to fall for you?" I said, shaking my head, as I tried to suppress my laughter.

"Because I'm irresistible," he said, placing a lingering kiss on the corner of my mouth.

I didn't know how he was able to do it with such a simple gesture, but again Bentley had been able to take my breath away.

"Yeah, I guess you are," I sighed.

"As much as I'd love to kiss you here all day we should probably get going. I'd like to make it to the cabin before the sun goes down."

"OK. If you insist," I agreed, pulling away from his hold.

"I do, but seriously though, do you really need all that stuff? We're only going for a few days."

"I know! I really tried, but I have no idea how hot or cold it's going to be. I just want to be prepared, that's all. After all, it can get pretty cold up in the mountains at night."

"I can think of plenty of other ways to keep you warm, Ireland," Bentley said, his eyes penetrating mine. "And, if I'm really being honest I'd rather you not bring any clothes at all."

His words left me tingling between my thighs. Two can play at this game.

"Well, if you'd like, we can leave that suitcase behind," I said, pointing to my pink, over-the-shoulder bag.

Bentley eyed me curiously. "OK. But why that one?" he asked, suspiciously.

"Because that one is full of my lingerie," I said with a wink, before retreating into the SUV as quickly as possible. I shut the door and burst into laughter. After several seconds, I looked in the rearview mirror and saw Bentley still standing behind the car with his mouth wide open.

Looks like I won this round.

"Are you one of these guys that only stops when his fuel tank is on E? Or am I allowed to ask for potty breaks? I asked as Bentley backed the Range Rover down the driveway.

"Depends," he said, without continuing.

"On what?" I asked.

"Are you one of those girls that has to piddle every hour? Because if that's the case then I'm most certainly the guy that only stops when we need to fill the gas tank," he smirked.

"No, I think I can hold it for more than an hour," I laughed, slapping him on his rock-hard chest. "Does that mean I can ask then?"

He sighed. "I suppose, but only because I like you," he said, taking one hand off the wheel and resting it on my thigh. It was such a sweet, romantic gesture. I knew it now more than ever that in just a few days this man had been able to find a way into my heart. I was going to tell him this weekend. I just needed to figure out how.

"SHAMROCK, ARE YOU hungry?" Bentley asked as he lightly tapped my shoulder.

"Maybe a little," I mumbled, opening my eyes. "Where are we?"

"I was running low on gas. We're almost through Ohio. I didn't want to wake Sleeping Beauty, but I thought you might be hungry. It looks like there's a Wendy's inside. Do you want to go in and eat, or do you just want me to grab you something?"

"I slept that long? I'm so sorry! I'm a terrible road trip partner," I groaned.

"I was probably drooling, too," I added, wiping the corner of my mouth. Oh god. You aren't going to want to take me anywhere ever again!"

"Ireland, relax. It's not a big deal. You were tired. I loved watching you sleep next to me," he said.

"I'm glad you felt comfortable enough to do that—," he paused before continuing. "I just assumed that after everything you might be a little hesitant about long car rides. And, for the record, I'll take you anywhere you want to go, Shamrock."

"Honestly, even after nearly twenty years, I still get nervous about getting in a car. I'm just as shocked as you are that I could fall asleep. I guess you just make me feel safe," I said with a sad smile.

He squeezed my thigh. From just that simple gesture, I felt my heart skip a beat. "You stay here while I top the tank off. I'll just run inside and grab something really quick so we can get back on the road."

"Sounds good," I said, slouching back down in the seat. Bentley had already finished pumping the gas and was already inside the restaurant before I realized I hadn't told him what I wanted to eat. Suddenly my stomach growled. I guess anything would do at this point.

I looked back up at the sound of the car door opening. Bentley handed me two large cups and a paper bag before he slid into the driver's seat.

Opening the bag, I was shocked to see only two large fries. "You remembered?"

"What? Large chocolate Frosties and French fries? That was our thing. How could I ever forget?"

"It's just that everyone else thinks it's disgusting when I dip my fries into the chocolaty goodness," I said, reaching into the bag for a thick-cut fry.

"Nope. I don't care how old I am, or what diet I'm on. I'll always indulge in a Frosty and fries. I even taught Tanner to double dip," he said with a shrug.

"Mmmmmmm," I moaned. "I haven't had this in a few years. It may actually be better than sex."

"You won't be saying that after this weekend," Bentley said, popping another fry in his mouth.

My heart fluttered in my chest and my cheeks immediately flushed at his admission. I quickly turned my head to look out the window. Finishing the rest of my fries in silence, I said a silent prayer that Bentley couldn't see the effect he was having on me.

Chapter Nine

JUST AS BENTLEY had hoped, we arrived at the cabin shortly before nightfall.

"It's getting chilly outside," Bentley said, as he came around to open the passenger door. "Why don't you go inside and make yourself comfortable. I'm going to grab our bags. There should be an extra key under the doormat."

I stood at the edge of the driveway for just a few minutes taking in the view before me. The exterior of the cabin was just as I'd remembered it. The woods behind the house had thickened over the last twenty years, but everything else seemed just the same. The two-story log cabin sat on the foot of a hill and if I listened closely enough, I could hear the sound of flowing water from the winding creek that ran just a few acres away.

Everything was so peaceful. In that moment, I didn't have a care in the world. I remembered what it felt like to be an innocent child. Glancing past the cabin, I noticed that the golden rain tree that Bentley and I always got "married" under was blooming with bright yellow buds. Squeezing my eyes shut, I envisioned my mother sitting on the wrought iron bench watching us say our "I dos." She was wearing a light blue sundress and her sun-kissed, blond hair was blowing in the wind.

Bentley walked up behind me and set the bags on the ground before placing a gentle kiss on the top of my head. I'd been so

lost in thought that I hadn't even checked for the key.

"Did Dad forget to set the key out for us?" Bentley asked, as he dropped my luggage at my feet. "No, I'm not sure. I haven't even checked for it. I was just taking everything in. I guess I just forgot how beautiful this place is. It's filled with so many memories."

"I've always loved this place," Bentley said. "Mom wanted to replace the stones out front with some fancy new siding a few years back, but Dad and I stood our ground. I don't ever want this place to change. She got her way on the inside though."

"We women usually find a way to get what we want," I said, nudging him in the side.

Just as Bentley had said, there was a spare key under the faded blue mat that sat just outside the squeaky, brown-metal screen door. Before I stepped inside, I turned back and took another look at the empty bench. A butterfly landed on the arm and I couldn't help but think my mom was still watching over us.

"Wow, remind me to tell your mom that I love what she's done with the place," I said, as we stepped into the entryway. "The hardwood floors are definitely an improvement over that seventies shag carpet."

"You know you loved the *Austin Powers* look," Bentley joked.

"No," I laughed, shaking my head.

"Let me guess. You picked out the hideous bearskin rug over there by the fireplace, didn't you?" I chuckled to myself remembering my earlier conversation with Katie.

"I bet you won't think it's so hideous when you're rolling around on it with me later," Bentley smirked.

"You just don't stop do you," I laughed. "I guess I should be grateful that it's here and not at your condo back home. Please tell me you didn't buy two."

"Nope, just this one. But, if you really love it, I'm sure Mom would be OK with us taking it home with us."

"No," I practically shouted, as I walked in to explore the rest of the cabin. "It can stay here. Ooooh, but can we take that back?" I asked, walking up to the sliding glass door and pointing at the hot tub which had been added to the covered deck out back.

I heard Bentley laughing at me as he rummaged around in the kitchen.

"Anything I can help you with?" I asked, walking into the newly remodeled kitchen fit for a five-star chef. The stainless steel appliances perfectly matched the tiled floor. In the middle of the room sat a huge island with bar stools that matched the cherry wood cupboards. Although this kitchen was every cook's dream, my favorite piece was the chef's rack filled with stainless cookware suspended from the ceiling.

"No, but it doesn't look like there's too much in the pantry. I don't think Mom figured anyone would be using the cabin again this season. We don't even have a box of mac and cheese.

"I think the little Chinese restaurant up the street should still be open. I can call for delivery. We can watch a movie or something."

"That sounds perfect. I'll go grab the wine from my suitcase."

"So, let me get this straight. We didn't pack any food, but you didn't forget the wine?"

"I don't understand the question. It's wine, Bentley. It's a necessity."

After just twenty minutes, we were curled up on the couch eating sweet and sour chicken, vegetable chow mein, fried rice and egg rolls straight from cartons.

"Why does Chinese food always taste so much better in these little white boxes," I remarked.

"I don't know, but it really does," Bentley said, reaching his fork over to take some chicken out of my box.

We channel surfed for a few minutes before stopping on an old episode of *Full House*.

"Are you sure this is OK? I remember how much this show used to annoy you."

"Whatever makes you happy is fine with me, Shamrock. Besides, I'm not really paying much attention to the television," Bentley said, reaching over to tuck a strand of fallen hair behind my ear.

Setting the food on the coffee table, I snuggled closer into Bentley's side. It wasn't really that late, but after spending the entire day in the car, I was exhausted. I woke up several hours later when Bentley stirred next to me.

"I think we both must have passed out," I mumbled.

"I think so, too. Do you want to head to bed? You can take the guest room—it used to be my room. Do you remember where it's at?"

"Yeah, I do. But, where are you sleeping?"

"I'm fine here on the couch. If you need anything just holler."

"I need you, Bentley," I blurted out so quickly I couldn't take back the words even if I'd wanted to. I bit the inside of my lip before continuing. "Come to bed with me—please."

I STEPPED INTO the nightie that I'd secretly slipped out of my luggage before coming back to the en suite bathroom to freshen up. I probably should have grabbed the entire bag, but I was just too exhausted from all the traveling. Since I'd forgotten to grab a pair of thongs to go with the ensemble, Bentley was going to get a nice surprise when he undressed me.

I reapplied my lip gloss once more before heading back to the bedroom—not quite ready to face Bentley. I wanted to open up and give myself one-hundred-percent to him, but I was still scared.

"Shamrock? Are you OK in there?" Bentley asked from the opposite side of the door.

"Yes, I'll be out in a second," I answered.

I took a deep breath and turned the doorknob. *There's no turning back now.* Walking out of the room, my eyes automatically zeroed in on Bentley who was busy rummaging through the drawer of the nightstand. Turning to face me, I noticed that he'd removed his shirt and socks and wore only a pair of low-rise jeans which showcased his washboard abs and mouthwatering V.

Looking up when he realized I'd entered the room, his jaw dropped and he began walking toward me—wanting to eliminate the distance between us. We met at the end of the bed, but Bentley stopped me before I reached him, holding a palm flat against my stomach.

"Stop right there," he growled. "I need to look at you."

I was on display. Bentley's eyes were greedily feasting on me and devouring every bit of me. Little did he know, he was consuming more than just my body. In that moment, I knew I was ready to give him all of me.

"This is a first for me," I spoke, breaking the silence between us.

He looked at me with confusion written on his face.

"I've never made love before," I continued, hoping to make him understand without actually having to say the words.

"You're not making any sense, Shamrock. I know you can't possibly be a virgin," he said, shaking his head.

I chuckled, "No, I'm definitely NOT a virgin. I don't think you understand what I'm saying . . . I've had sex before, but I've not made love before."

He paused for a moment before I saw the color in his eyes change before me. He swallowed and I watched his Adam's apple bob up and down before he spoke. "Are you saying what I think you're saying, Ireland? Do you love me?"

"I—." Bentley pulled me forward, only inches separated us now. I was certain he could feel the beat of my heart as it tried to leap from my chest. Before giving me a chance to finish my sentence, he placed his finger against my lips.

"Because I love you, Ireland."

A tear began rolling down my cheek before Bentley caught it with the pad of his thumb.

"Don't cry, Shamrock. You don't have to say anything. I just wanted you to know how I was feeling."

"I do, Bentley. I love you, too," I said as relief washed over me.

Before I had the opportunity to say another word, Bentley's lips crashed into mine. It didn't take long before he was nipping at my neck in an almost frantic pace. Gone was the slow and in control Bentley.

"Ireland, I want this to be perfect for you. I really do. But, I'm not sure I can control myself this time," he groaned. "If I'm being honest, I've had a horrible case of blue balls since I saw you last week."

As I chuckled at his admission, it was sweet that he was worried about my feelings and wanted to take it slow, but I wanted him—needed him inside me just as badly.

"We have all night to take it slow, Bentley," I whispered in his ear. "But right now, I just want you inside me. I want to feel you—all of you. And, I don't want you to be gentle."

"Well then, although this little number looks sexy as hell on you it needs to go," he said, referring to the pink lace negligee I'd packed for such occasions.

He nipped at my neck and reached for the hem, pulling it over my head. A hiss erupted from his lips as my lingerie pooled at my feet, leaving me completely bare and exposed before him.

"You're so beautiful, Ireland," he said with adoration filling his voice.

Parting my lips once again with his tongue, he trailed down my body with heated kisses. He clamped down on my nipple causing me to squirm and I could feel his hard shaft rest against my stomach as he paid close attention to each of my breasts.

Walking backwards in a heated frenzy, I soon felt the edge of the mattress behind my knees. Bentley lightly nudged my shoulder and I fell back onto what felt like a cloud of plush pillows. Spreading out before him, I waited for him to claim me. I wanted nothing more than to be his—forever. Scooting toward the head of the bed, I watched as Bentley unzipped his jeans. His pants fell to the floor, leaving him in only a pair of very tight boxer briefs—which weren't leaving much to my imagination.

I pointed at his very hard erection which had begun to pop out from the top of his briefs. "I think someone wants to come out and play," I giggled.

"It's not nice to laugh and point at a man's cock, Shamrock," Bentley hissed, as he began to crawl up the bed before coming to a stop and resting on his elbows so he was hovering directly above me.

"I was definitely not laughing at your cock, Bentley," I nearly panted, as I took my thumb and began rubbing it over the head of his dick. "I think the rest of him needs to come out," I said, as I moved my hand to the elastic band of the boxer briefs and tugged them down.

Bentley did some hot maneuver, resting his weight on one arm as he used the other to remove his boxers completely. Lying there with my mouth agape, I watched the rippling veins in his bicep.

I felt his hands trail from my navel down to my sensitive, and now very awake, core.

"Fuck. You're so ready for me, Shamrock" he moaned into my ear as he began working my pussy with his fingers. I felt my walls begin to tighten around them as he moved his thumb and rubbed over my clit in a slow, circular motion.

"Ahhhhhhhhh, fuck!" I screamed. "That feels incredible. So fucking good."

He claimed my mouth once again as I let myself go in what

had been my first, not self-induced, orgasm in months.

"Bentley, I need all of you," I begged as I felt his tip rub against my clit.

"Soon, Shamrock," he said, kissing me on my forehead before propping himself back up on his knees.

"Where are you going?" I asked.

"I need to grab a condom out of the nightstand."

"No, it's fine. I'm on birth control. Get back here."

"Are you sure? I'm clean. I was tested after everything went down with Staci. Do you trust me?"

I realized then that we'd still not addressed his past, but now wasn't the time. I knew he'd confide in me when he was ready. He needed to know that I accepted everything and trusted him completely.

"Of course, I trust you. I want you, Bentley. All of you."

With my request, Bentley plunged into me and I gasped at his sudden entrance. Only taking a moment for my walls to mold around him, he filled me completely and I rocked back and forth as he pumped himself in and out of me.

Bentley kept at a rigorous pace and after just a few minutes, I could tell by his breathing that he was getting close to his own release. He brought a hand down between us, taking a finger to rub my clit, as he continued to thrust his hard cock into my wet, slippery core.

Angling his body, he used his mouth to suck on my breasts. The double pleasure was too much and he soon sent me over the edge as I began to writhe beneath him, my walls tightening and spasming around his thickness. Slamming into me once more, Bentley groaned as he let go of his own release.

Lying in silence for several seconds, we both tried to catch our breath. The only noise came from the crickets chirping in the distance.

"I love you, Ireland. I love you so much," Bentley said, as he rolled over beside me, pulling me into his arms.

Bentley was completely serious when he said he planned on making love to me all night long. Our sex marathon went well into the early morning hours before we finally fell asleep wrapped around each other.

Chapter Ten

THE SCENT OF frying bacon along with sunlight beaming in from the large bay window woke me from the best night's sleep I think I'd had in years. Rolling over, I thought I'd find Bentley on the opposite side of the bed, but then remembered the bacon which obviously wasn't cooking itself. My stomach growled as I reached for my phone to check the time—eleven o'clock. Shit! I hadn't slept this late since my college days.

Sitting on the edge of the bed, I noticed that my suitcases weren't anywhere to be found. Bentley and I had been so tired when we arrived at the cabin that we'd left everything sitting in the foyer. The chilly hardwood floor left me wishing that I'd remembered to pack my warm fuzzy socks. I walked over to the dresser hoping to find something that I could slip on.

Opening the drawer and rummaging through a bunch of faded undergarments, I settled on a pair of M&M boxer shorts and a worn and tattered Super Mario Brothers T-shirt. Both items smelled like the bag of cedar chips that had been placed in the back of the drawer. Clearly these had both belonged to Bentley circa 1992.

Padding down the hallway, I found Bentley in the kitchen wearing nothing but the same pair of faded jeans from the previous night. His back was turned to me and from what I could tell he was flipping pancakes on the electric griddle. I quietly walked about behind him, very much enjoying my view. *I mean a sexy man, with an ass on which you could bounce quarters off, cooking in the kitchen? Who wouldn't enjoy that view?*

I put my arms around his sculpted shoulders and nuzzled into his back.

"Well good morning, sleepyhead. I'm sorry if I woke you," Bentley said, placing a peck on the back of my hand.

"You can wake me any day of the week if I get bacon and kisses. But, you didn't wake me. I can't believe I slept until eleven. I'm pretty sure I haven't slept this late since I was eighteen. You must think I'm such a lazy ass."

"No, I just like to think that I fucked you so thoroughly last night that you needed a few extra hours to recharge," Bentley teased, turning to face me.

"Actually, I am feeling pretty energetic," I said with a wink. "Feed me and there is no telling what I might be capable of doing."

Before I was able to say another word, Bentley was doubled over, laughing hysterically. "What the fuck are you wearing?"

"It's all I could find in the bedroom," I shrugged. "You don't like it? I thought I might take it home with me and make it a new fashion trend. It seems like everything else from the eighties and nineties is coming back. Why not the retro video game T-shirt and candy boxers?" I added, striking a pose.

Bentley pulled me into his chest. "You somehow are able to make anything look sexy, Shamrock. You want to know the best part?" he asked.

"What's that?"

"I can tell you aren't wearing a bra under that old T-shirt of mine. Want to know how I know?" he whispered into my ear.

"Hmmmm?"

"I can see your nipples pebbling under that thin fabric. They're just waiting for me to reach under there and pinch them." he said, sliding his hands under the shirt and gently rubbing the pad of his thumb over my pert nipples.

I felt my heartbeat increase and a wave of heat coursed through my core. Just as Bentley was lifting me onto the island, we were interrupted by the untimely sound of my stomach growling.

"You've seriously got to be kidding me right now," I groaned.

"I think someone wants food then sex."

"No, just ignore it. Sex first. I always need sex first," I encouraged, as my stomach rumbled again.

Bentley placed me back on my feet and turned to grab two plates out of the cupboard.

"As much as I hate turning down your request, we're eating. You need to keep your energy up for what I've planned for later."

"Is that a promise?" I asked, reaching for the plate of bacon.

"It's not just a promise, Shamrock. It's a guarantee."

"Mmmm," I moaned. "I think you were telling me stories when you said you couldn't cook. This bacon is orgasmic."

"Well I'm capable of cooking bacon and pancakes, but if you want eggs then you're on your own. And, the only thing in this room that better be giving you orgasms is me. Got it?"

"Aye aye, Sir," I said with a salute. "Seriously though, where did you get this food? I thought you said the cupboards were bare?"

"I've been awake for a few hours. I didn't want to wake you so I went out for a run and then stopped at the corner market for a few things on my way back."

"Well I'm glad you did," I said, stacking four pancakes onto my plate. "But, way to really make me feel lazy. Who runs on a Saturday?"

"I thought you weren't that hungry?" Bentley questioned, eyeing my plate of food.

"I never said I wasn't hungry. I just said sex was more important than food. But, since you insisted we eat then I'm going to go big. I don't believe in half-assing anything," I said with a playful grin. "Oh and could you please pass the maple syrup?"

"Oh Shamrock, I think that kinky mouth of yours is going to take some getting used to," he said, passing me the syrup. "Don't be afraid to let any of that dribble onto your chest. I'd love nothing more than to lick it off your rack later."

I nearly choked on my orange juice as Bentley began clearing the dishes from the table. It was like a constant game of cat and mouse between us. *And, if I'm being honest with myself—I'm quite enjoying it.*

AFTER DEVOURING THE breakfast that Bentley had made for us. I stood at the sink with warm water and suds up to my elbows.

"Why don't you hop in the shower. I'll take care of the rest of the dishes," Bentley said, coming up and swatting my rear from behind.

"It's fine. It's the least I can do after you cooked me all that amazing food. I don't think I could eat another bite for days. Besides, I thought we could save some time and just shower together."

"As much as I love that idea, I don't think it would be saving us any time and I promised my mother we'd visit around two this afternoon," Bentley explained, looking down at his watch. "And, since Sleeping Beauty didn't rise until eleven, we don't have much time."

"Fine," I groaned. "I'll make it quick."

I pulled a light, mint sundress and black shrug out of the suitcase that Bentley had already rolled into the guestroom and laid them out on the bed so I could quickly get dressed after stepping out of the shower. I decided to forgo washing my hair, opting to pull it back in a messy bun, in order to save a few extra minutes. After all, I'd been the one to sleep away most of the morning, so I didn't want us to be late to meet Bentley's parents. It'd been years since I'd seen Mr. and Mrs. Roberts. *Do I still call them Mr. and Mrs. Roberts? Or, are they just Martin and Rita?* I made a mental note to ask Bentley on the ride over to the house. I wanted everything to be perfect. I'd already told Bentley that I loved him and I didn't want anything holding us back now.

I was just about to turn the water off when the shower door opened and Bentley stepped inside—completely nude. My eyes widened as I took him in from head to toe. I saw Bentley naked last night, but only by moonlight. Bentley by daylight—just fuck me now.

"You're drooling, Shamrock."

"I'm what?" I stammered, unable to take my eyes away from his perfect V and light trail of hair which led to his already fully erect cock.

"Like what you see?"

"Mmmmmhmmmm."

"Eyes up here," he said, pointing to his own eyes.

I did as asked and stared into his big brown orbs. "I like what I see too, Ireland. If I failed to tell you last night, I think you're beautiful," he said, taking my mouth into his and sliding his hands down my already slippery front. "Fucking breathtakingly gorgeous."

"I thought you said we were going to be late," I mumbled, trying not to break the contact between us.

"I called my folks after I finished up the dishes and told them I had an important errand to run before we'd be there."

"Bentley, you shouldn't have lied to your mother."

"I didn't lie. I do have a very important errand I need to attend to—I just didn't tell her that errand was you," he said with a sly smirk. "She understood and told me to take my time and not to rush. And, since Mother knows best, I plan on taking my sweet time."

WE PULLED UP to Bentley's parents' house about two hours later than expected. Bentley really did take his mother's advice to heart—he didn't rush anything. After fully pleasuring me in the shower, he took his sweet time on the bed as well.

"We shouldn't have taken so long, Bentley," I said, as he opened the passenger side door and held his hand out for me.

"Would you relax? Everything's going to be fine. They loved you when we were kids and they're going to love you now."

"You don't know that. They haven't seen me in decades. What if they don't think I'm good enough for their son?" I asked, concern evident in my voice.

"First, I think it's adorable that this actually concerns you. I'm nearly thirty-five, you know. Hell, as Katie would remind me, that's nearly forty. This old man is capable of making his own decisions when it comes to the women he dates. But it doesn't matter anyways because they will love you. I mean, what isn't there to love? You've made a career out of helping orphaned children. You have a heart of gold. You're pure perfection from the inside out, Shamrock."

I chuckled, "I wouldn't go that far."

"OK, you're right. After last night and this morning, you're far from pure."

"Ireland, Darling, it's been far too long," Rita interjected, as we walked up the winding cobblestone path which led to the wraparound porch of their remodeled, historic plantation farmhouse.

Rita was just as lovely as I remembered. Her auburn hair was pulled back in a loose bun with a few curly tendrils framing her face. The pink skirt and ivory blouse she was wearing had me second guessing the linen sundress I'd thrown on, still probably wrinkled from my suitcase.

Bentley's family had never been hurting for money. Before his retirement, Martin had been CEO of a large southern banking corporation and Rita still owned a chain of successful, high-end clothing boutiques throughout Kentucky and Tennessee.

Money never defined who they were though. His family had always accepted my mother and me even though, as a child, I'd often worn hand-me-down clothes and my mother didn't drive the fanciest cars. We weren't poor by any means, my mother kept two jobs to ensure I never did without, but I didn't grow up with the same luxuries as Bentley.

"You're just as gorgeous as I remember and you look so much like your mother. I was always so envious of her beautiful blond hair and big green eyes," Rita added, kissing me on the cheek as we stepped onto the porch. *Shit! I'd forgotten to ask Bentley what to call his parents on the drive over. I'll have to play it safe and cross my fingers that I don't offend anyone.*

"It's good to see you again, too, Mrs. Roberts," I said, wrapping my arms around her.

"Don't be silly, dear. It's Rita. And, seriously, you really do have such a stunning glow about you."

Bentley turned his head and gave me a knowing look. So only I could see, he mouthed, "Freshly fucked."

My face flushed and I cleared my throat hoping Rita hadn't noticed the exchange between her son and me.

"Mom, stop fawning all over my girlfriend," Bentley interjected, attempting to take the focus off me. *Girlfriend? Did Bentley just refer to me as his girlfriend? I suppose it would be logical since we'd both said those three little words the night before. Was I ready to be Bentley's girlfriend?* Before I had too much time to dwell on the subject, Rita focused her attention onto Bentley.

"Jamie, I've missed you, son. Come give your mother a squeeze. If I'd known the only way I was going to get you down here was to go under the knife, I would have scheduled surgery years ago."

"Mom, stop it. I was just down here with Tanner and Staci at Christmas," he said, wrapping his mother in a firm embrace.

"That was three Christmases ago," she said, furrowing her brow. "And, we won't speak of that awful woman whom I never approved of again. But, I do miss my grandson. It's been too many months since we made it north to see you. I bet Tanner is getting so big. Hopefully you can bring him down to see his gam-gam soon."

"That was three years ago? You know I'm sorry, Mom. Things became hectic for a while—you know, with the divorce and all," Bentley said with remorse. "Tanner would love to come see his grandparents though. We'll have to Facetime when we get back to Michigan. I know he misses you."

"Hush. We won't have any further conversation about it. You have your Ireland by your side now. The way it was always supposed to be," she said, placing her hand on mine and giving it a gentle squeeze. "Now, you two head inside. I know Martin is just dying to see you both."

JUST AS RITA had foretold, Martin was standing in the foyer waiting for us to enter. He swooped me up into his arms, my feet barely touching the ground, before I'd hardly even stepped over the threshold.

"Well if it's isn't our little Shamrock all grown up," Martin said, placing me back on my feet. "You certainly have grown into a beautiful woman. My son sure is a lucky man." Everything was happening so quickly. My head began to spin. I hadn't seen Rita and Martin in nearly twenty years and in that moment, so many emotions and memories came flooding back. I'd always thought of Mr. and Mrs. Roberts as family. But after the accident, they'd been ripped away from me—just like everyone else

I'd loved. I took a deep breath hoping it would bring my sudden dizziness to a halt.

"You've got that right, Dad," Bentley interjected, sensing my unease.

"Martin, don't be rude, let our company come in and sit down," Rita said, pointing toward the living room.

"Yes, Rita is right. Where are my manners? Please come in and make yourself at home."

"I have cheese and crackers in the kitchen. Can I get you some iced tea, too?" Rita asked, as she began to exit the room.

"That'd be great, Mom. We'd both like some. Thank you," Bentley answered.

A few minutes later, Rita came into the room carrying one tray loaded with cheese and crackers, and with cookies, peanuts, trail mix and ham rollups. Martin wasn't far behind with two large pitchers, one with iced tea and the other filled with lemonade.

"Mom, did you invite the neighborhood and not tell me?" Bentley joked. "I thought we were having dinner shortly."

"Leave your mother alone, Son. I tried talking some sense into her when she was buying all of this at the market this morning, but she was just so excited that the two of you would be visiting. We don't get much company as Jamie lives so far north and Kevin is stationed overseas. She'll be laid up for a while after the knee surgery so I figured I'd let her get away with it just this once."

I popped up from the couch to help Rita. I don't know how her impending surgery had already slipped my mind. "Rita, is there anything I can help you with? How are you feeling anyways?"

"No, thank you, Ireland. Please sit back down and relax. Dinner is already in the oven. There isn't much else to prepare. My knee will be fine, dear."

Martin poured three glasses of iced tea along with a

lemonade for himself before joining his wife on the loveseat. I took a gulp and liquid came shooting out of my mouth.

"Shamrock, are you OK?" Bentley asked, patting me on the back—assuming I was choking.

My face reddened from embarrassment. "Oh my god. I am so sorry. I just wasn't expecting sweet tea. I forgot that it was a thing down here," I said on the brink of tears.

Instead of getting angry, Rita started to laugh. "It's quite all right. I should have warned you. I forgot you crazy northerners drink your tea without sugar. I could never understand the point of that myself. If you prefer tea without sugar why wouldn't you just drink water?" she said, shaking her head in confusion.

"Let me get a towel to wipe up," she offered. "The washroom is through the hallway and to your right if you'd like to clean yourself up."

After taking a few minutes to collect myself, I rejoined Bentley and his parents in the living room.

"Again, I am so sorry about the carpet," I said.

"Not another word of it, Ireland. You can't even see a stain," Rita assured me. "Well, since we know the sweet tea is out—that is what you northerners call it right—how about I pour you a glass of lemonade? Or, I did make up a batch of sangria. Perhaps you would prefer something a little stronger?"

"Actually, sangria sounds perfect."

Chapter Eleven

AFTER THREE MORE glasses of sangria, I was actually starting to feel pretty comfortable around Bentley's parents.

"Would you like another glass of the good stuff to go with dinner, Ireland?" Rita asked, as she began setting the table with four place settings.

"No, I think I've had more than enough, Rita. At this rate, Bentley will have to carry me out of here."

"I don't mind that one bit," he yelled from the den where he and his dad were watching an Atlanta Braves baseball game.

"James Bentley Roberts! Your mother can hear you," Rita shouted back.

"Sorry Ma!"

"It's really OK if you'd like another drink, dear. Just think of it as a fruit salad. I know that secret because that's the same story I tell myself," she explained, pouring herself another glass.

"Well, when you put it that way, it's kind of hard to refuse," I said, passing her my glass.

Rita and I chatted for a few more minutes before she called the men into the dining room for dinner.

Bentley surprised me a bit as he pulled my chair out from the table and gestured, like a true gentleman, for me to sit before moving it back into place.

"Your mother taught you well," I said with a smile.

"Can I tell you a secret," Bentley said, whispering in my ear.

"Of course," I said, trying to suppress my laughter.

"She's watching me like a hawk. When you excused yourself to use the bathroom, she told me she would kick my ass if I messed this up."

That was all it took for me to fully lose it. I doubled over in laughter as Rita walked into the room carrying a piping hot tray of homemade macaroni and cheese.

"What do you two find so funny?" Rita asked, setting the tray directly in front of me.

"Your son was telling me about the threats you made while I was freshening up. Thank you for having my back, Rita."

"Always, dear. Us girls have to stick together," she said with a sly wink.

"Did you hear that Dad? We don't even stand a chance." Bentley said to Martin who had taken a seat at the head of the table.

"It's best if you just smile and nod, Son. Surely you have learned that at your age," Martin said.

I could tell Bentley was getting a kick out of this exchange between his parents. "Please school me, Dad. What is your tip for a successful marriage?"

"Your mother is always right. Even if I know she's wrong— she's right," he said, placing a chaste kiss on Rita's cheek.

I really had missed this. I remember sitting at this very table several times as a child. Rita often agreed to watch me when my mother was at her second job so she wouldn't have to spend her paychecks on childcare for me. Mac and cheese night was always my favorite.

"Please help yourself first, Ireland," Rita said, motioning toward the tray of gooey pasta.

"It's OK. Someone else may go first."

"Don't be silly, dear. I made the macaroni and cheese just for you. I remembered it was your favorite. You especially liked the crunchy, Ritz cracker topping. I made sure to put extra on it for you."

"I can't believe you actually remembered that small detail," I said, surprise evident in my voice.

"We remember so much about you, Ireland. You've always held a special place in our hearts—all of our hearts," she said, giving her son a knowing glance. "We can't tell you how elated we both were when Bentley called us the morning after the wedding to tell us who he had run into. It's such a small world really. What are the odds that our Ireland is Gregory's wife's best friend and maid of honor? You two have almost come full circle—first as ring bearer and flower girl and now as best man and maid of honor. Now we just need another wedding," she added with a wink.

Bentley must have noticed the look of panic spreading across my face. "Let's not get ahead of ourselves, Mom."

"What? I'm just stating the inevitable," she said nonchalantly.

Thank god I hadn't been drinking sangria at the time or it would've ended up all over Rita's tablecloth. *Of course then maybe she wouldn't be speaking of the "inevitable."*

We made it through the rest of dinner without any talk of a wedding. At least a marriage between Bentley and me. We went on to tell Rita and Martin all about Katie and Greg's wedding. Hearing Bentley tell his mother about seeing me again after all those years sent chills up my spine. More than once, I wanted to fake an illness in hopes that we could head back to the cabin early and finish where we'd left off earlier in the day.

"You two have such a history with weddings. I remember your mother taking so many pictures of you two during your pretend nuptials."

"She did? I would've loved to see those," I said, with a hint of sadness. "I don't really have many photos from my childhood. Just the few tiny pictures in the locket Bentley gave me when we were kids."

"I wish I had them here, dear. I would love to see them again as well. I do believe there is a box somewhere back at the cabin though. You're welcome to look for it."

"Seriously, Mom? Is this your way of making Ireland clean out your old stuff?" Bentley chuckled.

"No, son. I just remember rescuing a box of photos among other things from the curb of Ireland's house after the new owners began moving in. Ireland had already gone into foster care, and I didn't have any way of seeing she got the items. I tried contacting social services, but they wouldn't give me any information—all that red tape, you know," Rita said, with a few tears welling in her eyes. "I always hoped she would come back into our lives, but after so many years I began to give up hope. I often considered tossing the box, but something always held me back. I realize now I was always right—you belong with us, Ireland."

I swallowed back the lump in my throat and reached across the table to hug Rita.

"You'll never know how much that means to me, Rita. For so many years, I've felt like I haven't belonged anywhere. Tonight, I feel like I truly belong. I feel like I'm home," I whispered, looking back at Bentley.

After I'd helped Rita wash up the dinner dishes and we were seated back in the living room, I could hardly focus on anything the rest of the evening. All I kept thinking about were the contents of that box and what might be packed inside. Bentley tried making small talk and including me in the conversation, but it was very evident my mind was someplace else entirely.

"Earth to Ireland," he said, waving his hand in front of my face.

"What? I'm sorry. I guess I'm just tired after the long drive yesterday. I do apologize," I said, sheepishly.

"No need to apologize, dear. Bentley, I think you need to get this girl tucked into bed. And, don't keep her up all night," she added with a wink.

"I don't know what you're talking about, Mother."

"Don't give me that nonsense, son. Your father and I were young once, too."

"OK, on that note, I think it's about time for me to get this one back to the cabin," he said, pointing in my direction.

"We'll stop by again tomorrow before you leave for the hospital," he said, standing to kiss his mother on the cheek.

WE ARRIVED BACK at the cabin shortly before nightfall. Bentley unlocked the door for me, before heading off to find some wood for a bonfire. I couldn't forget the box of childhood items that Rita thought might be stored in the basement of the cabin. I probably should've waited for Bentley, but instead decided to head down to the basement on my own. Hopefully he wouldn't feel I was overstepping my boundaries.

I opened up the door that led to the basement and flipped the light switch—darkness. Shit! A burnt out light bulb. I've never really been a big fan of basements. It seems like they're always cold, damp, dark and filled with creepy crawlies.

Deciding to grin and bear it, I placed my hand on the railing. I ran quickly down the stairs—each step creaking below my feet—my only source of light coming from the hallway upstairs. Reaching the bottom, I walked head first into what felt like the mother of all cobwebs. *What did I tell you about creepy crawlies?* I was going to itch for the rest of the night.

Pulling the silky strands from my hair, I soon spotted what appeared to be a lamp in the opposite corner of the room. I crept over to the light, careful not to trip in the darkness, and turned the switch—again nothing. "Seriously? It's like I'm in one of those cheesy horror movies. Jason is probably waiting for me on the other side of the room," I said to myself.

Just then, I heard a creaking sound coming from back near

the basement stairs. I bolted toward the steps, hoping it was just my imagination getting the best of me. I'd almost made it back to the landing when I ran smack dab into someone's firm chest.

"Ahhhhhh," I screamed. "Please don't kill me with your chainsaw."

The rock-hard chest began twitching and laughter soon erupted, making me realize I wasn't dealing with Jason after-all.

"Bentley! You're such an asshole. You scared the shit out of me. I thought you were still outside," I screamed, smacking him in the chest.

"I got back a few minutes ago. I called for you a few times, but you didn't answer. I saw the basement door was open so I came down to look for you. Why didn't you turn any lights on?"

"Gee, lights? Why didn't I think of that," I answered with obvious sarcasm in my voice. "None of the damn things work, Bentley!"

Reaching into his pocket, he retrieved his cell phone. He tapped on the screen a few times before his flashlight app opened, producing a stream of light.

"Huh, why didn't I think of that," I chuckled.

"I don't think the light bulbs are burnt out. It's a blown fuse, no doubt," he said, walking over to the circuit box. After dusting off the box and fidgeting around for a few minutes, the lights all came on.

"Just as I suspected," he said.

"Well, aren't you just Mr. Fix-it in the flesh," I said, reaching up to give him a quick peck on the lips.

"Does that mean I'm forgiven for scaring you?" he asked.

"Not entirely, but you're moving in the right direction," I said with a wink. "Now help me find this box that your mom said was down here."

After pulling down dozens of boxes and finding nothing but old Christmas decorations, we'd almost called it quits. I was just about to tell Bentley to call off the search when I spotted two boxes, with Bentley's name written on them, on the top shelf of an old workstation.

"Do you think those could be the boxes," I asked, sounding hopeful.

Bentley pulled down the first one, wiping away a layer of dust before opening the lid. I almost couldn't believe my eyes. On the very top, lay the green checkered blanket from my childhood that I remembered so well. I reached for it and immediately brought it up to my nose. It was probably just my imagination, but I swear I could smell the floral perfume that my mother always wore, mixed with the woodsy scent that I always assumed was my father's cologne.

"I can't believe this has actually been here for nearly twenty years," I said, tears now streaming down my cheeks. "I don't know how I can ever thank your mother for this. It means so much more to me than words can even begin to express."

"She knows, Ireland. I'm glad you accepted my invitation to come here this weekend," he said, gently running his fingers through my hair.

Under the blanket were four photo albums. Setting the box on the floor, we knelt beside it before searching through the albums. I opened the first and was shocked to see pictures from my parents' wedding.

"I remember my mom showing me these when I would ask her questions about my dad," I said, running my fingers across the old prints. "I didn't think I would ever see them again."

Also inside the box was my father's old police badge as well as photos of Bentley and me as children and then as teenagers. In some we were playing dress up and in others we were helping to build the tree house with Martin and my Uncle James.

My favorite was a small album filled with photos from our homecoming dance from my freshman year of high school. I looked so young in the photos—so carefree. I'd nearly forgotten that time in my life. So much of my teenage and young adult years had been filled with heartache. It wasn't until I'd graduated from college and became a social worker that I actually found true happiness again—and even then something, or someone was still missing. I was starting to believe that Bentley always was that missing someone.

"Young love," I said to Bentley who was looking over my shoulder. "I didn't have a care in the world."

"Your date was one lucky dude. He's a stud, too, if I must say so myself," he laughed.

"Full of yourself much?" I said, rolling my eyes. "I was so skinny. Someone should have fed me a cheeseburger."

"You were just as beautiful then as you are now, Ireland," he said, his eyes wandering to the dip in my shirt. "But, if I'm being honest, I do really love this more filled-out version of you."

"I'm sure you do," I laughed.

"I remember how excited I was when I found that dress. I wanted to look perfect for you," I reminisced, lost in my own memories.

Bentley and I had hidden our relationship from our friends and parents for years before finally telling everyone the truth. I wanted to scream it from the rooftop from the moment Bentley and I kissed in the tree house, but he thought it would be best if we kept it as our little secret. I always thought it was because I was two years younger than Bentley and he didn't want to admit to his friends that his girlfriend was just a kid. He insisted that he just didn't want anything to change between us.

I was beyond ecstatic when I began my freshman year at Jefferson High and Bentley asked if he could officially call me his girlfriend and escort me to the homecoming dance. I'd waited for what seemed like forever to hear those words come from his mouth. Our friends acted surprised, but I knew they really weren't. The two of us had been nearly inseparable since we'd met nearly seven years earlier.

Bentley's mother was so excited when we told her. I think she was already envisioning our wedding and her future grandchildren while my mother was a bit hesitant about the entire romance.

I remember I nearly had to beg her to allow me to go the homecoming dance with Bentley.

"Please, Mom," I begged, every night for nearly an entire week. "Please say you'll let me go to the dance with Bentley. This is like a dream come true for me."

"I just think you should go to the dance with your girlfriends, Ireland. You just started high school. You shouldn't be in a serious relationship right now. You'll have plenty of time for that stuff when you're older."

"Mom, I've loved Bentley for as long as I can remember. If you won't let me go with Bentley, then I'm not going at all."

"I hardly think you know what love is Ireland, but if you're so sure you want to go to the dance with Bentley then I'll allow it. But, you WILL come home immediately after the dance. I don't want you out late, or going to any of those parties afterward."

Although I wasn't happy with her rules, she at least was letting me go to the dance and I wasn't about to argue with her.

"Thank you, Mom," I said, relieved. "Can we go shopping for a dress this weekend? I've saved my allowance. There's a dress in the window of Mrs. Roberts' boutique that I've had my eyes on for weeks. She's been holding it for me."

"Yes, I'll see if I can take the day off on Saturday and we can go. I've got some money set aside for a special occasion such as this, though. I don't expect you to spend your money."

Just as she promised, Mom and I went to the boutique that weekend to try on dresses. After trying on about eight different styles and sizes, I went back to the first dress I tried on—the lavender, knee-length party dress with the sequined bodice.

I can still remember the look on Bentley's face when he picked me up for the dance. He was dressed in a tuxedo with a vest and tie that matched the color of my dress. I giggled thinking that his mother had something to do with his choice of wardrobe. If it had been up to him, he would've picked me up wearing a pair of faded jeans and his worn football jersey.

"You look beautiful, Ireland," he said, securing the purple and white corsage of roses and carnations on my wrist.

"I remember thanking your mother for trusting me with you before we left for the dance," Bentley said, breaking through the memories. "You were so beautiful, Ireland. I couldn't wait for you to be at my side for every dance we ever had—homecomings, proms, college formals, weddings. We were so young. We had a lifetime of memories to create."

"I'm just thankful for the ones we do have," I said, resting my head on his shoulder.

"And, the ones yet to be created—including this one," he said, taking the album from my hands and setting it on the floor beside us, before capturing my lips with his.

The next thing I knew, Bentley was using his entire body to lay me back on the floor.

"I can't get enough of you, Ireland. I need to have all of you," he growled.

With those words, I lifted my hips from the floor and began unzipping my jeans and, in no time at all, Bentley stripped them off me. His mouth was soon planted on me again.

Starting at my neck and working his way down, he stopped to linger at my breasts before licking and teasing my navel. I wanted his mouth to pleasure me—to send me into spiraling bliss. My core tingled in anticipation for what was to come. While pleasuring my body's every inch with his tongue, his fingers found the elastic waist of my panties and gave them a yank. Bentley's sense of urgency only intensified the rising heat between my thighs.

"I can't believe you just ripped my panties," I panted. "But, if I'm being honest it was hot as fuck."

Bentley chuckled before responding, "I'm glad you approve. But, now it's my turn to be honest—I think you're hot as fuck."

Before I could respond, Bentley began placing sweet kisses on the inside of my thighs. His day-old stubble tickled my inner legs, causing me to writhe beneath him. Bentley took that as a cue, moving up from my thighs to gently suck on my clit.

With each lap, he brought me closer to reaching my own euphoria. Feeling my muscles tightening and constricting, my orgasm intensified, coursing through my body. Letting me catch my breath, Bentley began placing soft pecks all the way up my torso and breasts before consuming my lips with his.

"I think you need to lose some clothes right now."

"Well, what do you suggest we do about that?"

"I have a few ideas," I said, as I sat up and slowly began unbuttoning his shirt.

My breath hitched ever so slightly at the sight before me. Even though I'd already seen Bentley naked and we'd already given ourselves to each other, the sight of his sculpted six pack that led right down to that mouthwatering V on his hips still could steal my breath away.

I slid the shirt from off his shoulders and ran my lengthy fingernails down his chiseled abdomen and the thin line of hair which adorned his chest. Deepening our kiss as I loosened his belt, I lowered his khakis. His hard erection sprang free from the band of his boxer briefs. Quickly standing up, he dropped his pants and briefs and stepped out of them, tossing them over to my pile of clothes.

Before rejoining me on the floor, I rolled out of his way so I could take control this time around. I was now the one on top, holding his wrists down, with my head buried between his thighs. I loved every view of Bentley—from every angle, but watching him at my mercy brought out a little of the tigress in me.

I freed Bentley's wrists and reached under his body to gently cup his firm ass. Pulling him in closer, I practically unhinged my jaw, trying to take in all of him. He reached out and began fondling my breasts, as I continued to work his cock with my mouth.

His groans only urged me to take in even more of him as I began to work his swollen tip with my tongue. I slowly licked circles around his crown as he began to squirm beneath me.

"You're going to be the death of me, Shamrock. That feels so fucking good."

Knowing Bentley was on the brink of his own release, I took as much of his length in my mouth as I possibly could and let my hands begin to massage his balls. He slowly rocked his hips back and forth before I noticed his pace begin to quicken.

"Ireland, I'm going to come. You need to roll over. I want to be inside you when I come."

Knowing I wanted to taste him on my lips, I ignored his request and quickened my pace. Groaning he knew he'd lost this battle, pumping himself into my mouth a few more times before I could taste his cum on my lips. As he slowly sat up and watched, I licked every last drop of his essence from my mouth.

"Oh Shamrock, you're so naughty," Bentley said with a wink.

"You loved it," I sassed.

"I did love it, but you didn't do as I asked. Now I need to punish you," he said, lightly swatting my behind.

Before I had time to react, Bentley flipped us over and straddled me once again. Using his knee to spread my legs apart, he positioned himself at my entrance. I could feel the heat of his cock at my pulsating center.

"I love you so much, Ireland. I've waited my entire life to say those words." His confession drifted in the night air, as he filled me slowly with his hard length.

My body didn't take as long to adjust to him this time; we were now as one with each stroke. Not rushing tonight as he had the day before, he slid himself in and out of me at a slow, rhythmic pace, our bodies rubbing together in their own perfect melody. I was nearing my second release of the night, when I felt his thumb begin to rub my clit. That was all I needed to come unhinged. I cried out as Bentley thrust into me again before collapsing on my chest in his own release.

Chapter Twelve

BENTLEY AND I were still entwined in each other's arms when something on the floor caught my eye.

I rolled over to get a closer look at the aged wood board. "I can't believe our names are still legible," I said, my finger tracing the outline of the engraving. "I remember the day we did this."

Bentley + Ireland
Forever

Bentley rolled over in my direction to see what I was talking about. "I'd completely forgotten about that," he chuckled.

"Didn't you have a weird name for this thing?"

"Yeah, we all called it the 'Love Plank,'" he chuckled, lost in memory. "Mom and Dad started the tradition then Uncle James and Aunt Char added to it. I wanted to be just like him so we carved our names on it, too."

"I remember," I laughed. "We snuck down here after everyone else had gone to bed. I thought you wanted to make out. It surprised me a little when you only wanted to carve our names into the floor."

"If memory serves, we made out after we finished our little graffiti project," he said, pulling me into his chest and kissing the top of my head.

"We did," I laughed. "I probably pouted. I had you wrapped around my little finger."

"I guess some things never change," he whispered into my ear.

Upon further inspection, I was surprised to see Bentley's son's name engraved underneath ours.

"Isn't Tanner just a bit too young to have his name carved on there?" I questioned. "And, who the heck is Spike? You know what, maybe it's better if I just don't ask."

"Pfft," Bentley sniggered. "I would say that he was a little too young if we hadn't been nearly the same age when we carved our names onto the plank. Besides, Spike is just our old dog."

I couldn't help the laughter that escaped, "You let him carve his name with the dog's? You know that's permanent, right? That poor kid is going to be so embarrassed someday. He's never going to bring a girl down here," I nearly choked, trying to suppress my snickering.

"Exactly. That's why I was perfectly OK with letting him do it," Bentley chuckled.

Shaking my head, "You're so evil, Dad."

"And, you love this evil dad," he reminded me.

"I do."

Have I told you today that I love you, Ireland?"

"You have, but it's OK to tell me again," I sighed.

"I love you. I love you. I love you. How's that?"

"Perfect," I said, rolling around to face him. I wanted to bring something up and I wanted to be looking him in the eyes when I did.

Here goes nothing. "I noticed you never carved your name with Staci's," I said, biting the inside of my lip.

"I don't think I ever brought her down here. I never wanted to share you with her. I wanted the memories of us just to stay between us," he admitted.

"What happened between you two?"

Bentley pulled away almost as soon as I'd spoken the words. I instantly regretted my question.

"I'm sorry. Forget I ever asked."

"No. No, it's OK. You deserve to know," he said, inhaling deeply. Rubbing his forehead, he exhaled before continuing, "Things had been distant between us for quite some time. I probably should've seen the signs. Maybe I had, but didn't want to admit it to myself."

I rested my head against his bicep, hoping our close proximity would encourage him to continue. "I did love my wife. We may have been young and we may have rushed into marriage because of Tanner, but I took our vows seriously. I always wanted the same kind of marriage that my parents had. Growing up, I always thought that that was going to be us someday. It took me awhile to move on after you left, but when I met Staci I really thought she could be my forever."

"You know I didn't want to leave, right?"

"I know, Ireland. I'm not telling you any of this because I blame you, or because I think it's somehow your fault. You obviously couldn't control the circumstances any more than I could. Truth be told, you had a lot more to handle than I ever did. I can't even begin to imagine everything you went through—or how you felt."

Clearing my throat, I hoped Bentley would continue with his story because I wasn't ready to share mine—not yet.

"Anyways, I'd been working a lot of overtime. Greg and I had just opened the firm. It took countless hours to successfully grow our business. Staci said she understood—even held my elbow at all the corporate functions. Little did I know, she was actually using those same functions to find her next fuck."

"She cheated on you?" I asked, stunned by his admission.

"She did more than cheat on me. I don't think she'd been faithful the entire time we were married—maybe even before."

I shook my head in confusion, "I'm not following. That's a

pretty heavy accusation. How can you be sure?"

"I guess I can't be one hundred percent sure, but all the signs were there. I recently found out that she got pregnant on purpose, too. She told me she was on birth control. I was young, naïve maybe. I didn't have any reason to question her."

"How do you know? Why would she do that? She was so young, too."

"She admitted as much. She knew my family had money and she wanted into my mother's social circle. I suppose my name meant more to her than I did."

"I'm so sorry, Bentley. I had no idea."

"It's OK. I haven't told many people and don't even think Greg knows the entire story. I guess I'm a little embarrassed about the entire situation, since I couldn't even keep my own wife satisfied."

"You can't possibly blame yourself for her infidelity!" I nearly yelled.

"I don't know," he shrugged. "Maybe if I'd stayed home more and not worked so much."

"Bentley, you can't possibly believe that's true. You just told me that she was only with you for your family's money and that she hadn't been faithful since before you were married."

"She admitted that she thought she could make our marriage work. She would give it her best in order to eat at all the fancy restaurants, ride in limousines, and be showered with expensive diamonds. But then once she had Tanner, she got bored being at home alone with him all the time while I was working to build the new firm. It's sad, but my son and I weren't enough for her. She wanted to go out and play so that's what she did."

I didn't even know what to say, so I just let Bentley continue talking.

"She acted the role of the doting wife to perfection. She liked to attend the fancy parties and rub elbows with the other wives. I always thought she was bored by them, but as it turned out, she was meeting other area businessmen at these functions and fucking them on the side.

"That's where I caught her—in the act—at my last corporate function. I'd been looking all over for her when I finally decided to check and see if she'd gotten sick in an upstairs bathroom. I was shocked when I opened the door to find my wife with her skirt pulled up to her waist and one of my colleagues ramming his dick into her. It's an image that will forever be engrained in my mind."

"I can't even begin to imagine the pain that must have caused. She didn't deserve you, Bentley."

"I was pretty bitter for a while, but soon realized more than anything that Tanner needed me. He was the one hurt the most by the divorce.

"I think we're finally in a decent place now, though" Bentley continued, sighing. "He took it really hard when I left. He blamed me for the longest time—I don't know, maybe he still does to some extent."

"Did you tell him? Maybe if you tried explaining the situation to him—maybe he'd see that it wasn't your fault," I suggested. "After all, he's not a child and now old enough to handle the truth."

"No."

"Why?" I questioned. "I don't understand why you would take the blame for her."

"I'm not taking the blame for her. He just worships his mother. She can do no wrong in his eyes. Honestly, I don't want to ruin that for him. And, you're wrong about one thing—you're never old enough to handle that kind of truth. It would absolutely crush him. Hell, it absolutely crushed me. Besides, she may have gotten pregnant for all the wrong reasons, but she definitely loves that boy—we both do. And, we want nothing but the best for him."

"But what about the way he looks at you, Bentley? I still

don't understand why you insist on protecting her."

"Just drop it, Ireland. Things are fine between Tanner and me now. Time will make it even better."

"Trust me, Bentley. I know better than anyone that sometimes time isn't on our side." I instinctively reached out and grabbed his hand. Partially to comfort him and partially to remind myself that he was still there.

"Please, Ireland, let me do this my way. You don't have children. You can't really understand."

Bentley's words brought tears to my eyes. He'd never been so abrupt with me before.

"I'm sorry. I didn't mean it that way. You'll be a great mother someday, Shamrock. I just meant that I know my son and what he needs—just like one day you'll know exactly what our children will need."

"Our children?" I said hesitantly, wiping the tears from my eyes.

"Yes," he said. "I hope that's not too presumptuous. I know we've only been back together a short time, but I know I want nothing more than a future with you, Ireland."

"I'd like that too," I said, resting my head on his chest. And, it was true—I was really starting to like the idea of a future with Bentley.

AFTER RETREATING UPSTAIRS, Bentley went back outside to start the bonfire as I began rounding up ingredients for S'mores. We'd left his parents' place before dessert, and after the go-round with Bentley in the basement, I was actually getting quite hungry. As I was rummaging around the kitchen for the skewers, Bentley came back in the cabin soaking wet.

"Don't tell me it's raining," I pouted.

"Not raining. I just decided to jump into the river with my

clothes on," he said, as thunder clapped in the distance.

"You're a jackass," I laughed. "How do you explain the thunder then?"

"Such harsh words! I just said what you told me to say! I can't be blamed for following your instructions," he said, pulling me into his body.

"Stop! You're getting me wet," I squirmed.

"That's what she said," he smirked, placing a kiss on my forehead.

"You didn't just say that . . . Are we eighteen now?"

"We can be. Are we role-playing now? Is that your fantasy?" he whispered into my ear. Just then the lights flickered before everything in the cabin went completely dark. "Crap! Maybe you should hold that thought while I start a fire in the fireplace. And, maybe we should skip the S'mores tonight."

"Actually I saw this recipe on Pinterest for a S'mores dip, using a cast iron skillet, and I think if we're careful then we can pull it off," I suggested.

"Pinterest? Is that the chick-website with all the recipes and decorating shit?" he asked.

"It's a little more than that, but yes. Actually for a man, I should probably be impressed that you knew that much."

"What can I say? I'm a pretty impressive man, Shamrock."

"Oh my god. You're ridiculous. Now would you go get the logs before we freeze to death in here," I asked, massaging down my arms trying to warm myself.

"Would you rather I keep you warm?" Bentley suggested.

"Well, yes, I always want you to keep me warm, but I also want chocolate so can you please go get the logs."

In a matter of minutes, Bentley had retrieved the logs and had started a roaring fire in the fireplace. I opened the bag of chocolate chips and dumped them in the skillet before topping it with the large, fluffy marshmallows. Bentley stole one from the bag and stuffed it in his mouth.

"Mmmmm, I'd forgotten how great these things taste," he said, stuffing his mouth with another marshmallow.

"If you eat them all then we won't have any left for more dip," I said, pulling the skillet out of the flames.

"We don't need any marshmallows. I can just drizzle the plain chocolate all over your body," he said, placing his finger in the melted concoction.

"Wh—What are you going to do with that," I asked, my pulse beginning to quicken.

"I'm going to dab a little here," he said, smearing chocolate on the corner of my mouth.

"Mmmmm," I groaned. "And, then what are you going to do?"

"And, then I'm going to lick it off before smearing a little down here," he said, his voice thickening, as he licked the edge of my mouth before dabbing chocolate at the base of my neck.

Before I knew it, Bentley had me stripped naked, as he drizzled and licked a trail of warm, melted chocolate from my clavicle down to my navel.

He stopped to pay extra attention to each of my nipples. Nipping and sucking, before working his way down the length of my torso. He dipped his fingers back in the chocolate and drew another path down to the inside of my thighs before smearing the rest of the chocolate on my bare pussy.

Bentley had turned me into his very own candy-dessert bar and I was enjoying every last minute of it.

Chapter Thirteen

AFTER BENTLEY AND I returned back to Michigan following our long weekend, he immediately caught a flight back to Tennessee in order to stay with his parents for a bit longer after his mom's surgery. I wanted to stay with him, but I had responsibilities at work. Luckily, Greg was able to cover for Bentley, and anything that he couldn't handle, Bentley could do remotely.

It'd been almost two weeks since I'd seen him, and although we'd talked on the phone every night, I was missing him like crazy. Bentley's flight was scheduled to arrive at four in the afternoon and I'd made arrangements to leave work early in order to pick him up at Metro airport. As I was glancing at the files on my desk in order to handle my last case of the day, Susan appeared in the doorway.

"Hey Susan, is there something I can help you with?" I asked, glancing up from the paperwork of a young boy whose mother had just died of an apparent heart attack.

"Hi, Ireland," she greeted. "I hate to do this to you on such short notice, but as you know we have the outing scheduled tonight at the family fun center for all the children and foster families in our system and two of your co-workers have gone home with food poisoning. They were both scheduled to work the event tonight, but I doubt they'll be available after all. Is there any way you could come help for just a few hours?"

Glancing down at the clock on my desk, I responded, "Susan, I've already been approved to leave early and take this evening off. I'm supposed to pick up my boyfriend at the airport in two hours and was going to meet with this last case and head out of here. Isn't there anyone else who can take the shift?"

"I've tried everyone else, Ireland. I really am asking you as my last hope," she sighed. "I'm afraid if you can't work then I'll have to cancel the entire event."

"You don't need to cancel the event. I'll be there. I'll let Bentley know that there's been a change of plans."

"Thank you, Ireland. You really are a lifesaver. I owe you one," she said, retreating from my office.

I'd grabbed my cell from my purse and had begun typing a message out to Bentley when Susan came back into my office.

"Sorry to bother you again, but I just had a thought," she said. "Why don't you bring your boyfriend to the event with you?"

"That's sweet of you to invite him, but we were planning on spending the evening at home with his son. I'm sure Bentley wouldn't want to leave Tanner at home alone since he's been gone for the last two weeks."

"Bring them both," she said. "We have the entire place reserved. I'm sure his son will love it there. My kids are probably about his age and they think it's better than Disney World—although they've never actually been to the real Disney World."

"OK, I'll see what he thinks. Thanks for the invite," I said with a smile.

INSTEAD OF ME picking Bentley up at the airport, he decided to take a cab home to pick up Tanner and then meet me at the family fun center for an evening of batting cages, bumper boats and go-karts. It wasn't the relaxing night at home that I'd planned on, but at least I would be spending time with Bentley. I hadn't seen Tanner since the night at my place either, so I was happy to be able to spend more time getting to know him.

I was stirring three, large bowls of punch when I felt a pair of strong arms embrace me from behind. "I've missed you," Bentley whispered into my ear, placing a gentle kiss at the base of my neck.

"I've missed you, too," I said, turning to face him. "But we should probably keep this PG-rated because of our audience."

"I'm sure there's a broom closet around this place somewhere," he suggested with a wink.

"You're crazy! I'm not doing it in a maintenance room at my work function with children—including YOUR son—in the next room! Actually, on second thought—you're not crazy, you're disgusting!" I laughed.

"Fine! But just know that every time I look at you, I have disgusting thoughts running through my mind."

Smacking him on the chest, I said, "I'm going to pretend you didn't just say that. And, where is Tanner by the way? I haven't seen him."

"We'd barely made it through the door when he saw a group of his friends from school. I gave him some cash and told him he could find me on the bumper boats with you."

"Why the bumper boats?" I questioned.

"I figured it would be my best chance at seeing you in a bikini," he said, shrugging.

"You don't wear a bikini on bumper boats," I said, shaking my head.

"Wet T-shirt then?"

"No," I smirked.

"Well damn. But, you can't blame a guy for trying," he said, pulling me toward the climbing wall.

"Where are we going?" I asked. "You know I'm not climbing. I hate heights."

"Come on. I'll be right behind you. I won't let you fall, and you'll be strapped in a harness anyways."

"Can't we do something on the ground? Like the go-karts, or putt-putt?" I whined, sticking out my bottom lip.

"But if we do something on the ground then I won't have the chance to look up your shorts."

"James Bentley! You're on a roll tonight."

"I can't help it. I've been without you for two weeks. I'd been dreaming of a car quickie all day until you texted me with the change of plans."

"I think you can wait a few more hours," I said, giving him a peck on the lips. "Besides, your son is walking about with what appears to be a little, lady friend."

"Hi Ireland," Tanner said, waving at me.

"Hey bud, what's going on? It's been a while."

"Not too much. Just getting ready for school to start. We still need to have that Madden rematch."

"You name the time and place and I'll be there. I'll even bring the snacks."

"Awesome! Dad, when can Ireland come over?" he said, looking up at Bentley.

"Anytime she wants, Son. But, first, why don't you introduce your friend?"

"Oh right, Dad this is Sierra. Sierra this is my dad."

I knew I'd seen this girl before. She was one of the twins who I'd talked with the weekend following Katie's wedding. I didn't recognize Sierra right away because, fortunately, from what I'd read in her case files, she'd been placed in a good home with her sister following the death of her parents and we weren't required to intervene any further.

"Hi Sierra," I said. "Do you remember me? I'm Ireland. I was the caseworker who met with you a few weeks back. How's everything been for you and your sister?"

"Hi Ireland. I do remember you," she said with a slight smile.

"It's actually been OK. We're living with a really nice family now. Thanks to you. I think they're actually going to try and adopt us."

"That's fantastic news," I said.

"I didn't know you knew my dad's girlfriend," Tanner interjected. "That's really awesome that you were able to help Sierra, Ireland."

"She's actually helped most of the kids in this room, Son," Bentley said with pride in his voice.

"How do you two know each other?" I asked the kids.

"Sierra just started at my school and she's in my grade. I saw her as soon as we got here. Sierra thought she recognized you so we thought we'd come over."

I could tell that Tanner was crushing over this girl while it seemed that his father was totally oblivious to the entire situation.

"Well, we're glad you two came over," I said, patting Tanner on the back. "Your dad and I were just about to go play a game of putt-putt, so would you two like to join us?"

"We were? I thought we were rock climbing," Bentley said.

"Definitely putt-putt," I chuckled.

After talking it over in a whisper with Sierra, the two decided to join us.

WE DECIDED TO break off into a girls' team and boys' team. As we were nearing the end of the course, Sierra and I were beating the boys by an extremely wide margin.

"Dad! We can't let Ireland win again!" Tanner yelled from across the green.

"Yesssssssssss!" I shouted, as my ball rolled through the clown's mouth and into the hole.

"Hole-in-one," Sierra shouted, jumping up and down.

"Ireland, you're so good at this!"

"I can't take all the credit. My best friend is pretty competitive. She's the one who taught me the art of putt-putt." I laughed. "It all comes down to the windmills. If you can master those then you pretty much have a win in the bag."

"Is that all it takes?" Bentley said, pulling me into his side. "Why don't we let the kids finish our game. I have something I want to give you anyways."

"Well, you know I love presents," I laughed.

"You kids got this?" Bentley asked, as we started toward the bench just a few feet away.

"We're cool, Dad," Tanner shouted in our direction.

"If you ask me, I think Tanner has a little crush," I said, sitting down.

"I don't even want to think about it," Bentley said, rubbing his temples.

"Relax, Dad. You've done a good job. He's a smart kid."

"I hope so, but enough about the kids," Bentley said. "I saw this in one of Mom's boutiques and it had your name written all over it."

Bentley pulled a velvet box from his pocket. Knowing it wasn't the right size to hold a ring, I secretly breathed a sigh of relief. As much as I was enjoying my time with Bentley and was warming up to the idea of spending my life with him, I knew it was still too soon for something so serious.

"Open it," he encouraged, placing the box in my palm.

I opened the box and inside lay a beautiful platinum locket, similar to but more extravagant than the one Bentley had given me when we were kids.

"This is beautiful, but you didn't need to get me anything," I said, softly.

"I know I didn't need to, but I wanted to," he responded. "Take a look inside."

I opened the latch and inside were two pictures of Bentley

and me—the first taken inside the photo booth at Katie's and Greg's wedding and the second taken inside the cabin just a few weeks back.

"I love it so much!" I said, smiling from ear to ear. "Seriously, Bentley, this is the best gift you could've ever given me."

I cuddled into his arms as we sat under the stars watching Tanner and Sierra finish their game of miniature golf.

"Young love," I cooed. "Isn't it the cutest."

"You're really trying to kill me with that, aren't you?" he laughed.

Chapter Fourteen

Six months later

I WAS ENJOYING my Saturday morning, lounging in bed and watching old reruns of *Friends* when I heard the doorbell. Rolling out of bed, I padded to the door without even stopping to check myself in the mirror.

"Who is it?" I yelled through the door.

"It's your bestest friend in the entire world. Now open your damn door because my hands are full and I'm about to spill your latte all over."

"All you had to say was latte and I would've opened the door even if you'd told me you were a serial killer," I laughed, helping Katie with her haul.

"Holy shit. Why do you look like you just got your ass out of bed?"

"Because I did," I shrugged, sheepishly.

"You know it's after noon, right?" she asked.

"Yeah, what's your point?"

"My point is you're over thirty and you're still in bed at nearly one o'clock in the afternoon. I didn't think that was acceptable behavior after college."

"Eh, you only say that because you have a small alien growing inside you who probably got you up to pee before the sun came up," I said, placing my hand on her tiny baby bump. "Am I right?"

She chuckled, "Yes, sadly, you'd be correct. I just hope my bladder returns to normal after this child arrives. I'm only two-thirds done and I already feel like my body will never recover."

"You know you're not the first woman to give birth, right? Never mind, don't answer that." I said, rolling my eyes.

"Shut up!" Katie retorted. "I'm so going to laugh at you when Bentley knocks you up! At least then you'll understand what I have to put up with."

"Well that'll never happen. Sorry, sister."

"That's what you told me when I said you were going to marry the man six months ago, too. Do you remember that?"

"And, I'm not married, or even engaged. Bentley and I haven't even talked about it. We've only been together for six months. You're acting all sorts of crazy today."

She cleared her throat before responding, "First, don't ever call a pregnant woman crazy. Secondly, you might want to get used to the idea of marrying that man and pretty quickly, because I believe your boyfriend has big plans for tonight. He asked me to bring you that box and made appointments for us at the spa. The dude even handed me his credit card and didn't set any limitations. It's a platinum card, too. I think he means serious business."

Until she pointed it out, I hadn't really paid much attention to the big white box she'd brought in and set on my couch. "Are you going to open it, or are you trying to burn a hole in it with your eyes?"

Lifting the lid, I carefully pulled back the white tissue paper. I gasped at the most beautiful dress I'd ever seen.

"Have you already seen this?" I asked Katie, as I carefully removed the gown from the box.

"I mean there's a possibility that I took a peek," she said with a wide grin. "Your man has better tastes than I would've ever given him credit for. I guess he can design more than just buildings."

"Seriously, this dress is really more like a piece of art than clothing. I want to frame it. Should I even wear it?" Bentley really had outdone himself. The fitted dress was a black chiffon, floor-length evening gown with cap sleeves and a scoop neckline and featured stunning silver beading. The same beads embellished the sheer, plunging open back.

"Don't be ridiculous! You are most definitely wearing it. And, then you're going to keep it safe until I'm skinny again and can wear it." I eyed her ginormous boobs suspiciously without saying a word.

"Fuckin' A! They're never going to be a normal size again, are they?" she sighed, throwing her head back in a dramatic fashion.

"Afraid not, beautiful." I said, patting her on the shoulder.

KATIE AND I spent a refreshing afternoon at the spa. She used Bentley's credit card to treat herself to a prenatal massage while I enjoyed a hot stone massage. We both indulged on a mani-pedi, but Katie just watched as I got my hair and makeup done—saying she didn't want to have to hand over her firstborn after Bentley caught a glimpse of his American Express statement.

Returning to my place, she helped me into the black gown from Bentley. I was in the bathroom touching up my makeup when I heard her call out from the bedroom.

"Where did all this bling come from?" she yelled, rifling through my jewelry box.

"I bought most of it for myself through the years," I shrugged, walking back into the bedroom. "A few of the new pieces are from Bentley. He got me the diamond studs and matching bracelet for my birthday."

"You must have like twenty necklaces in here. I didn't think counselors were paid that well. I need to look into changing my career," she chuckled.

"Ha! Trust me, it's really not that great. I just don't spend all my extra cash on shoes and purses like other people I know. I never thought I'd have a boyfriend to buy me sparkly things so I just saved and bought them for myself."

"Well, soon you're going to have a huge, sparkly rock to wear on your finger," she squealed.

I exhaled deeply before responding. "We don't know that for sure. Can we please talk about something else? Like what shoes am I going to wear with this dress?"

"You are going to say 'yes,' right?"

"I need a purse, too," I yelled, as I started throwing shoes, hangers and belts from the bottom of my closet.

"Ireland, you need to cool it. Just sit down and take some deep breaths," Katie encouraged.

"Why am I not ready for this? I love him," I cried, placing my head in my hands. "I've always loved him. This should be the happiest day of my life and instead I'm terrified."

"You aren't terrified of spending the rest of your life with him, sweetie. You're afraid of losing him. Trust me, you aren't going to lose him so just be happy," she said, rubbing large circles on my back.

"I can't believe I'm admitting this, but you're right," I said.

"I'm sorry, I don't think I heard you correctly. Can you repeat that, please," she said with a playful wink.

"You heard me, asshole. Seriously, though, you're right. After all, we aren't even sure what Bentley has planned for tonight. I should just go and enjoy my boyfriend and this beautiful dress," I said, standing to twirl around, while admiring it.

AS I WALKED into Iridescence, I couldn't help but feel overwhelmed at everything that Bentley was trying to do for me tonight. This was the prom that he should've escorted me to nearly twenty years ago. He'd thought of everything including the purple and silver balloon archway and twinkling, white lights.

As I waited for Bentley to arrive, I took a moment to take in the view of the city below me and accepted a glass of champagne from the maître d'. I hoped it would help to calm my nerves as I anticipated the big question that Katie was expecting Bentley to ask me tonight. Was I really ready to marry him? Was I willing to finally let my heart become completely vulnerable? I did love him—I was sure of that. I just wasn't sure I could actually accept his proposal right now. We'd only been together for six months. What about Tanner? He'd accepted me as his dad's girlfriend, but would he accept me as his stepmother? Where would we live? Would I have to sell my house? Would he sell his?

"Calm down, Ireland. If he gets down on one knee then you'll know the answer," I said out loud. "You'll have to know the answer."

I looked down at the diamond-encrusted watch that I only wore on special occasions and noticed that I'd been waiting almost an hour. Bentley had texted me while I was in the limousine that he had to make a quick stop at the construction site, but that he'd only be a few minutes. He should be here by now. I opened the black clutch that I'd borrowed from Katie and pulled out my cell phone, assuming I'd just missed a text message from him—nothing.

It wasn't like Bentley to not tell me if something had kept him and he'd be running late. "I guess he just wants to be fashionably late," I mumbled to myself, as I scrolled through my contacts before clicking on his name. Straight to voicemail. I tried again thinking that maybe he'd tried calling me at the same time. Voicemail again. After three failed attempts, I was starting to worry. Just as I was picking up my phone to try again, I saw

Katie's face flash across my screen.

"Hey! I didn't expect to be hearing from you so soon. Is everything OK with the baby?" I asked.

"Ireland! There's been an accident. You have to get a taxi and get to Mercy Hospital immediately," Katie screamed into the phone.

"Who? What? Katie you're scaring me! Who's been in an accident?"

"Ireland, it's Bentley. He was at the construction site with Greg and he fell from the scaffolding. Greg called for help and the paramedics were there within minutes, but he said it's not good. He thinks he hit his head pretty hard, probably broke some bones and there could be some internal bleeding."

I didn't hear much after Katie said Bentley's name. It was happening to me all over again. I was losing the one person who I finally had let myself love. Why was every person I'd ever loved taken from me? What had I done to deserve this?

"Is he alive?" I asked, swallowing back my tears. It was the only question running through my head.

Katie paused and I feared the worse.

"Katie, just tell me. I need to know."

"They were able to find a pulse, but he's very critical right now. Do you need me to come and get you?"

"No, I'll be fine. I'll be there as soon as I can," I said, trying not to hyperventilate.

"I don't believe you. I'll be there in fifteen minutes. I love you."

"I love you, too," I said, disconnecting the call.

I crumpled to the floor and sat there sobbing—flashbacks of their accident playing through my mind.

"Mom, can I get a ride home with Bentley?"

"I don't think that's a good idea, Ireland. He just got his license and I'm not sure I'm comfortable with you riding with him yet. Besides, you just spent the last two hours at the movies with him. Uncle James

and Aunt Char came over to take us out to dinner anyways. We'll just come pick you up at the theater on our way to the restaurant."

"Fine, but can Bentley meet us there?"

She sighed before answering, "Ireland, I really think you're spending too much time with him."

"Mom, we've always spent a lot of time together. How is this any different than when I was ten?" I questioned, even though I knew very well how it was different. When I was ten I still thought of Bentley as my best friend who still possibly had cooties. Now I think of him as my boyfriend who I like to kiss—a lot.

"Ireland, it's different and you know it. Please don't argue with me."

"Fine, but he's insisting on staying here until you get here."

She sighed before answering. "I wouldn't expect any less of him. I may not like the idea of you having a boyfriend, but I'm glad that Bentley seems to be such a gentleman. We'll be there in about ten minutes. We'll meet you in front of the building. I love you, Ireland."

"I love you, too, Mom," I said before hanging up the payphone.

Bentley waited with me outside the theater for what seemed like forever. We'd found a bush on the side of the building that we could see around, but kept us out of view. Bentley stole a few kisses when we didn't think anyone was watching.

"Do you know how long we've been waiting here?" I asked.

Looking down at his watch he answered, "I think about twenty minutes, give or take five."

"That's strange. My mom said they'd be here in ten minutes. It's not like her to be late."

"Do you want me to take you home? Maybe you misunderstood and she was still waiting for Uncle James and Aunt Char to show up. He does have a habit of being late."

"I think she would actually kill me if she showed up here and I had gone with you. I would definitely be grounded for my entire life."

"I think you're being dramatic, Shamrock. I think she would understand. Besides it's getting chilly out here and it looks like it's about to rain. I really think I should just take you home. Maybe we'll pass them on the way there and we can turn around."

"OK, you win, but can I borrow a quarter and call her once more before we leave. I used my last one when I called her the first time."

Using Bentley's quarter, I tried my mom once more, but she didn't answer the call. I figured she was on her way to the theater and waited another five minutes with Bentley before agreeing to let him take me home.

Opening the door to Bentley's Ford pickup, I jumped into the passenger seat. Once I was seated, he reached over and buckled my seatbelt before placing a gentle kiss on my nose.

"I need to keep my Shamrock safe," he said with his dimply-grin before putting his keys in the ignition.

John Michael Montgomery's "I Can Love You Like That" began playing over the radio. Bentley began singing the words and scooted closer to me on the bench seat.

"Who sings this song?" I asked.

He looked at me like I'd grown two heads. "You can't live in Nashville and not know that's John Michael Montgomery. I think you should be kicked out of the city—maybe the entire state," he exclaimed.

I couldn't help the laughter that escaped me. "Then keep it that way," I giggled, tears now streaming down my face.

"Cute, Shamrock. Real cute," he said, singing the words even louder. He held out his hand, linking his pinkie finger with mine before putting the truck in drive.

We'd made it about five minutes down the road when Bentley had to pull over to let an ambulance pass. Just seconds later, a second ambulance came speeding by.

"There must be a bad accident up ahead. I see several emergency lights. Must be the reason your mom was late. They probably couldn't get through."

As we approached the scene I saw metal and glass strewn about the roadway. I looked for the vehicles and then saw the tires of an upturned car in the ditch. On the other side of the road, I could make *out the top of what appeared to be a mangled, red Oldsmobile Alero. It looked as if a car had crossed the center line and hit the other head-on.*

Paramedics were using the Jaws of Life to remove a body from the backseat of the car. Two gurneys with white sheets covering what I assumed were bodies were rolled next to one of the ambulances. Police were stopping traffic in both directions and were roping the entire area off with yellow caution tape. Chills ran up and down my spine thinking about the unfortunate victims and their families.

"Yikes. This looks pretty bad. I think they only cordon off the area if there are fatalities," Bentley said.

With Bentley's words, I began to really take note of the scene before us.

"Bentley, was that a red Alero that was in the ditch?"

"I think so. Why?"

"Doesn't Uncle James drive a red Alero?"

"Fuck! I think so."

The tears began to pool in my eyes as I came to the shocking realization my entire family was deceased—gone.

The following days are all a blur in my memory. I'd lost my entire family and was taken away from the love of my life all within the matter of minutes.

"Ireland! Ireland, you need to get up! We need to get to the hospital. Greg has the car running by the door. We can get to Mercy in just a few minutes," Katie yelled, interrupting me from my thoughts.

"I can't do this again, Katie. I can't lose him, too. Not again," I sobbed as she gathered me up from the floor.

Chapter Fifteen

TWO DAYS HAVE passed since Bentley's accident—two days have passed since he's opened his eyes—two days have passed since I've heard his voice—two days have passed since I've heard nothing but the gentle beep of his heart monitor reassuring me that he's alive.

He was in surgery when I arrived at the hospital on Saturday night. The surgeons were able to stop the hemorrhaging and inserted a chest tube to reinflate his lung. The swelling in his brain had diminished, but the attending doctor said we wouldn't know the extent of his brain trauma until he regained consciousness—if he regained consciousness. At this point, it was all a game of wait and see. They were talking about my boyfriend's life as if it were a game of Chutes and Ladders.

After Bentley was out of surgery and the doctors had stabilized him, they'd allowed me to stay in his room. I was horrified when they first let me see him. Katie and Greg waited for me out in the ICU lobby as I went into Bentley's room alone. He lay lifelessly in his bed. Everything was motionless except for the rise and fall of his chest with each beat of the ventilator which was the only thing keeping him alive—and here with me.

The nurses brought in some extra blankets and pillows for the window seat that could convert into a bed if I wanted to try and get some sleep.

The next morning, the orderly brought me a bag with Bentley's belongings. Most of his clothes were ruined from the paramedics having to cut through them, but his jacket was still in one piece. I removed it from the bag and brought it to my chest, breathing in his familiar, crisp scent. For a moment, I could avoid the sterile smell of the hospital and pretend none of this was happening.

As I was laying the coat down next to me, I felt something hard in the pocket. Investigating further, I pulled out a black, velvet ring box. Opening the box, I noticed it held a stunning French-set halo diamond. The sunlight cascading through the window reflected off the diamond, creating a dancing effect on the white, hospital room walls.

I cried as I realized that Katie had been right as usual. With everything that had happened in the last twelve hours, I'd forgotten what the previous night was supposed to symbolize. I'd forgotten that I was ever scared to be Bentley's wife. Truth is, I wanted nothing more than for him to be my future. I loved Bentley and I wanted nothing more than to be his wife. I just hoped that he knew that as well as I did.

"Yes," I whispered to myself. "I would be honored to be your wife, James Bentley Roberts."

I slipped the ring on my finger and held it in the light for a few minutes before placing it back in the box. I wanted to keep it on my finger more than anything, but I always wanted nothing more than for Bentley to be the one to place it there. I slipped the box back in Bentley's jacket pocket, saying a silent prayer that he would wake up and everything would be the way it was meant to be.

THE NURSES COMING in and out of Bentley's room to check his vitals had kept me awake most of the night. Katie had begged me to go home and get some rest, but I couldn't leave Bentley when he was still unconscious and in the ICU. With less brain swelling, the doctors had been able to ween him from the sedatives and were able to remove the ventilator. It was a step in the right direction, but Bentley was still unconscious. I wanted nothing more than to see his chocolaty eyes and hear his smooth voice.

I'd just received some news of my own and although I should've been ecstatic, all I felt was an emptiness. I was alone all over again.

As I reached for Bentley's limp hand, I hoped he could hear me. "I don't know how to tell you this, so I'm just going to say it," I said, pausing to take a deep breath. "I'm pregnant. You're going to be a daddy again."

Using the back of my hand, I wiped the tears from my eyes. I don't know why, but I guess I hoped that my sudden admission would bring Bentley back to me.

I'd been throwing up ever since Bentley had been taken into the ER two nights before. At first, I thought it was just my nerves and stress, but as the hours went by, I began to suspect it was something a little more. Even the scent of my favorite latte had me running for the bath-room. And, since I'd hardly eaten a bite in over forty-eight hours, I was fairly certain I could rule out food poisoning.

I'd snuck off to the hospital gift shop when Katie and Greg had come to sit with Bentley. I'd lied to Katie and told her I was going to the cafeteria to grab a bite to eat. Since she and Greg had been hounding me about eating, they were more than happy to sit with Bentley for a few minutes. After everyone had left for the evening, I used the adjoin-ing bathroom to take the test.

I'd always been so careful not to allow this to happen. I never want-ed children—primarily because I was afraid that something might happen to me someday. I didn't want my children to go through the pain that I went through—I didn't want them to have to grow up feel-ing alone. And, yet here I was. Alone on a cold bathroom floor waiting for two tiny, pink lines to appear.

I sat and stared at my phone, waiting for three minutes to pass before looking at the white test stick. I took a deep breath before glancing at it.

"Looks like I'm going to be a mommy," I said to myself, rubbing my invisible baby bump. I walked back out into the room and sat in the chair beside Bentley's bed. Wishing again that he would wake up, now more than ever.

I was surprised to see Katie standing in the doorway. "Katie! What are you doing here? I thought you and Greg had left for the night," I said, trying to hide my surprise.

"We did, but we were nearly home and I realized I'd left my purse in the room," she said. "See, there it is," she added, pointing at the black Michael Kors bag sitting in the corner of the room.

"You could've called. I would've kept it safe until morning."

"My prenatal vitamins are in it. I don't have any extra at home and I didn't want to miss my daily dose. They're important, you know," she said, eyeing me suspiciously.

"How much did you hear standing over there?" I asked.

"Enough," she admitted, sheepishly.

"Oh." It was the only response I had.

"I wasn't trying to eavesdrop. I swear."

"It's OK. I know you didn't mean any harm."

"Why didn't you tell me you thought you might be pregnant? I would've sat with you while you took the test."

"I know, but since Bentley was in no condition to hold my hand through it, I figured I should do it alone," I sighed. "I hope you understand. You know I wouldn't have been able to keep it a secret for long."

Her next question surprised me. "Are you happy?"

"Yeah, I think so," I said, biting the inside of my cheek. "You were right. He was going to propose. I found the ring in his jacket pocket last night. I told him 'yes.'"

"Oh my god! Why didn't you tell me earlier? My girl is getting married and having a baby!"

"Not exactly. Bentley never got a chance to officially propose. He needs to wake up and ask me first," I said with a half-smile.

"He will and he will. You just wait and see. You've waited long enough for your HEA."

"You read too many of those cheesy romance novels," I chuckled.

I'D JUST DRIFTED back to sleep in the chair beside Bentley's bed with his hand in mine when I felt him stir. My head snapped up and I saw his gorgeous brown eyes looking back at me.

"Bentley!" I shrieked, tears streaming down my face. "You're awake. Thank god you're awake."

Removing his hand from mine, he stared at me in confusion.

"I should go get the doctor," I said. "Don't try to talk, or move too abruptly. Your lung collapsed during the accident and they had to insert a chest tube. They took you off the ventilator earlier today so your throat is probably quite sore. And, your left arm is also broken and in a sling."

Standing up, I pressed the nurse's call button. Bentley continued to stare at me blankly—void of any emotion.

"I'm sorry that was probably a lot to throw at you all at once. Just try and stay calm while we wait for the doctor."

"My name's James," he gasped, wincing from the pain. "And, Staci? Where's Staci?"

"Shh. Bentley, baby, you must be confused. Why would you want Staci here?"

"My wife? I need Staci. Please bring Staci," he said, barely above a whisper. Before I had a chance to question him any further, he'd drifted back to sleep.

Another day passed and Bentley only woke up for that brief

moment. After going over Bentley's most recent tests along with his asking for Staci, the doctor believed Bentley was suffering from Retrograde Amnesia, a form of post-traumatic amnesia.

We wouldn't know the severity of his concussion and symptoms until he woke up again, but from what I'd researched online in the hospital room, his recovery could take from just a few hours to several months. Katie had begged me to stay away from Web MD, because my mind would conjure up the worst possible scenarios, but I had to get some answers—even if it did worsen my anxiety.

From what I'd learned, Retrograde Amnesia was a loss of memories that were formed shortly before the injury. Since Bentley woke up and immediately asked for Staci, without even acknowledging me, it left me to believe that he didn't remember me—at least the grown up me. I feared that in Bentley's current mental state, I was still just a distant memory of a fourteen-year-old girl—definitely not his now pregnant fiancée.

I'd done as Bentley had requested and asked Staci and Tanner to both come and stay in his room. I wanted everyone there when he woke up again. Since he woke up briefly yesterday, the doctor suspected he would be regaining full consciousness soon. He'd also removed the chest tube so Bentley was resting more comfortably.

I was sitting in the window seat when I overheard Staci talking to Bentley.

"Jamie—Jamie, open your eyes for us again? Come back to us," she begged.

I knew she was only trying to help, but I couldn't hold back the tears. I should be the one holding his hand, talking to him, asking him to wake up—to come back to me. She'd already had her chance to love him and to be loved by him and she blew it. I didn't even want to think about the possibility that she would be given a second chance.

As I was wiping the tears from my eyes, I heard Bentley's

raspy voice.

"It's OK, I've come back to you—to both of you. I'm here now," he whispered.

My head snapped up. *To both of you?* Does he remember me, too? My initial excitement was short-lived when I looked over to his bedside and remembered Tanner was sitting there with Staci. Bentley had come back to Staci and Tanner. They were getting their second chance as a family and I was losing everything I'd ever loved—again.

I wanted to leave the room and escape this unfolding nightmare, but instead I tortured myself and watched their happy reunion.

"Oh, thank god you're awake," Staci said in relief. "I'll go get the doctor. He should probably examine you now that you're awake."

"Just give me a minute with you," Bentley pleaded. "I just want to hold you."

"Jamie," she said, pulling back. "Do you remember anything—anything about the accident—about falling?"

"No, I didn't even know I'd fallen. It's all pretty fuzzy. I only remember waking up briefly and calling out for you. The nurse said she would get you."

"The nurse?" she questioned.

"He thinks I'm the nurse?" I said to myself, my tears now falling faster. "Isn't that just rich."

"Jamie, she isn't your nurse. That's Ireland," Staci tried explaining.

"Ireland?" Bentley asked, confusedly. "I don't understand. Why is Ireland here?"

"Because you were planning on marrying her, Jamie." I had to give Staci some credit. At least she was acknowledging my role in Bentley's life and not just dismissing me all together.

"Staci, you aren't making any sense. How can I marry another woman when you're my wife?"

"She's not your wife. She's a cheating whore. You love me. You wanted to marry me! You bought me a ring!" I wanted to shout all of that and more, but instead I sat quietly as tears continued cascading down my cheeks.

"Jamie, we haven't been married for nearly a year," she said, biting down on her lip. "I really think I should go get the doctor now."

BENTLEY LOOKED AS if he'd seen a ghost. The little color that had returned to his cheeks in the days since the accident had vanished in just a matter of seconds. His void expression shattered my heart into a million tiny pieces. I wanted nothing more than to be this man's wife, and now he didn't even know me. And, our baby. I had more than just myself to think about now. I needed to get a breath of fresh air before I broke down in the middle of Bentley's hospital room.

Staci was out in the hallway talking to Bentley's doctor when I exited the room.

"Doctor, can you tell us what's going on?" I interrupted.

"Ireland, can't you see we're in the middle of a conversation?" Staci said, obnoxiously.

"Yes, I see that, Staci. I was just hoping for a little more information on Bentley's condition. That's all. I would think you could understand that since I am his fiancée."

"Excuse me, ladies. I'll let you two work this out while I go check on my patient," Bentley's doctor said, walking into Bentley's room.

"You're not his fiancée, Ireland. Jamie doesn't even remember you. You've no right to his medical information. You're insignificant. He still thinks we're married and I intend on keeping it that way."

"Then why did you remind Bentley that he was going to

marry me?" I said, placing emphasis on calling him Bentley.

"I wanted to see his reaction. If he'd remembered you at all then I would've let you two continue with this little rebound romance that you have going on. I mean you have to realize that's all you are—just a fling until he comes back to me."

I took a deep breath; I wouldn't let this woman take me down. "We're much more than a fling and you know it. Besides, you didn't want Bentley all those years that he was your husband. Why would you want him now? Do your fuck buddies not have money? Don't buy you expensive presents?"

"I made a mistake, Ireland. I let the best man who'd ever been in my life get away. I still love him. He doesn't remember the past year and I don't intend on reminding him. I suggest you do the same."

"Why would you believe I wouldn't tell him about your indiscretions and about our relationship?" I shot back. "Are you sure you're not the one who was hit in the head?"

"You won't tell him because you can't hurt him, Ireland. Do you want to be the one to tell him about my affair? You saw the way he looked at me when he opened his eyes. He loves me, Ireland. Do you want to be the one who breaks his heart, and for no reason? He's already been through enough. Do you want to hinder his recovery? He wants his family. He wants Tanner and me—not you."

Her words made me sick. I needed to get out of the hospital. I felt the walls closing in. I wasn't going to make it much longer. I took a quick glance into Bentley's room and saw Tanner sitting on the edge of the bed as the doctor checked Bentley's head wound.

He needed to know the truth—about everything, but now was not the time. I needed to take a timeout to reevaluate my life and figure out if Bentley still fit into it.

Turning back to face Staci, I said, "Fine. You get your way—for now. But, this is far from over."

"Whatever you want to tell yourself to make it better, honey" she said snidely. "But, we both know the truth, Ireland. You won't be back in Jamie's life again."

I turned and walked away, not even acknowledging Staci's parting words. Even if Bentley wanted to be with Staci, I had a baby to think about now. My son or daughter needed to know their father. I owed them that much, didn't I? Or maybe I needed to save them from the inevitable hurt of loss.

Before I'd even exited the hospital, I stopped and let myself slide down one of the bare walls to the floor. Resting my head against the concrete slab, my tears couldn't stop. How had my life so drastically changed in less than seventy-two hours? I don't know how long I'd been sitting on the cold, hard floor when a voice interrupted my thoughts.

"Miss? Miss, are you OK? Should I get a doctor?" a familiar-looking, older woman asked.

"No, no thank you. I just have a lot on my mind and needed a breather," I explained, getting up from the floor and dusting off the back of my jeans. "Thank you for your concern though."

"I don't mean to intrude, but would you like to talk about it?

I gave the woman a weak smile before responding, "Thank you again, but I think I need to handle this one on my own."

"OK, but if you change your mind I work in the hospital gift shop. I'm the one who sold you the pregnancy test yesterday. I don't know your situation, or even how the test came out, but I have a feeling that something's troubling you," she said. "Oh dear, there I go again. Just ignore me, dear. Have a lovely afternoon."

"You do as well," I said, giving her a tired smile as I turned to exit the building.

Chapter Sixteen

TWO WEEKS HAD come and gone since I'd walked through the hospital doors—leaving Bentley in Staci's care. I learned from Katie and Greg that Bentley had been released a week earlier, and was recovering nicely, though his memories still hadn't returned.

He'd gone back to the home he'd shared with Staci and Tanner before the divorce. From what Greg could tell, they seemed happy, but they still encouraged me to go see him. Each morning I woke up telling myself that I would visit him—tell him the truth about the baby, but each day passed—ending with my crying myself to sleep.

Katie had given me the name of her obstetrician and I'd scheduled an appointment to make sure everything was on track with my pregnancy. I'd had a lot of morning sickness, and had taken a lot of time off from work. I was starting to wonder if I was really slacking on my job responsibilities because of the early pregnancy complications, or because I didn't want to keep updating everyone on my status with Bentley.

For as much as I tried to keep my coworkers out of my personal life, that all went out the window the day I'd taken Bentley with me to the rec center. Not only had the kids taken to him that day, but every woman—and possibly one man—in my office had as well.

Today was the big day. I was meeting with Dr. Rhoads for the first time and would hopefully learn my due date. I'd just gotten out of the shower and was toweling off my hair when the phone rang from the bedroom. Running from the bathroom, I dove onto the bed reaching for the phone.

"Hello," I answered, without even looking at the screen.

"Hey pretty mama. Today's the big day, right? Do you want me to go with you to your appointment?" Katie asked.

I felt a twinge of disappointment that it was Katie calling. A part of me had hoped that Bentley's memories had suddenly returned, but as each day passed I was starting to believe that might never be the case. "Ireland, are you there?" she asked when I didn't respond right away.

"Yeah, I'm here. Sorry, what were you saying?"

"You were hoping I was Bentley, weren't you?"

I sighed before answering, "I'm such a horrible best friend. You know I love you, right. I just . . ."

Katie cut me off before I could even finish my sentence. "I'm only giving you a hard time, Ireland. You're not a horrible best friend. I can't blame you for wanting that hunk of a man instead of this ginormous pregnant lady."

"Stop it. You're beautiful," I scolded.

"Yeah, I am, aren't I?" she said with a laugh. "Seriously, though, do you want company at your appointment? I'd be happy to tag along."

"Nah, I'll be fine flying solo. I'm sorta used to it after all these years of singledom."

"Shut up. You know as well as I do that I didn't let you do anything alone—ever. And, just so you know, I'm not taking no for an answer. Besides, I have a craving for a big bowl of chicken alfredo and one of those cannoli thingies. So, we're doing lunch at the little Italian bistro near the doctor's office after your appointment—just so you know," she said with a giggle.

"OK, fine. But, I'll probably just get a ginger ale and watch you eat. I still can't keep anything down."

"Make sure you tell Dr. Rhoads. She gave me a tiny magic pill that took all my morning sickness away almost instantly. The only bad part, I think I gained like twenty pounds in a week because I couldn't stop eating all the food," she said, chewing in the background.

"You're eating a doughnut, aren't you? I said, trying to stifle my laughter.

"Don't judge. You know what they say about karma," she said. "You'll understand in about five months. It's like all the food just talks to you. Well, maybe except the broccoli and asparagus. That healthy shit never talks.

"You're crazy. I need to finish getting ready. But since you're insisting on going to this appointment with me then you can swing by and pick me up in about an hour," I said, ending the call.

EVERYTHING CHECKED OUT perfectly at my appointment. Dr. Rhoads didn't feel as if my morning sickness was cause for alarm and prescribed some of the magic pills that Katie had mentioned. I'd taken one almost immediately after having the prescription filled and already felt like I could actually keep food in my stomach.

We'd arrived at Antonio's and were seated by the door almost immediately. Katie was already drooling over the menu when I remembered the ultrasound picture I'd stuffed in my purse on the way out of the office.

"I can't believe I actually have a picture of my baby," I said, staring at the sonogram image. "Hello, Little Bean. Mommy already thinks you're so beautiful."

"Isn't it the craziest. Wait until you're farther along and they do the three-dimensional one. My boy seriously looks like an alien-child."

"That's only because he's all scrunched up in there. He'll be so handsome when he's born. You'll see."

"I think you're having a girl," she said, sipping on the water the waitress had just delivered to our table.

"What makes you think that?" I said, skeptically.

"Isn't it obvious? I'm having a boy so you will definitely be having a girl. It's destiny that they'll get married someday."

"So my child is still resting comfortably in my womb and you already have her married off to your alien-son?"

"You just said my son would be handsome! And, you totally said 'her!' You think it's a girl, too!" she yelled, clapping her hands.

"That's not what I meant. I was just going by your warped scenario. And, your son is an alien if he goes after my daughter!"

Just then I felt a cool breeze on my back as the door to the restaurant opened and closed.

Katie looked up and her jaw immediately fell to the ground. "Oh shit," she said.

"What's wrong?" I asked, fearful that she was going into early labor. "Do you need me to call Greg?"

"No, no. The baby's fine."

"What is it then?"

"Don't look now but Bentley just walked in with Staci and Tanner," she explained.

I knew she told me not to look, but it's like in a slasher movie when the killer comes on the screen—you know you shouldn't look, but you can't stop yourself. I slowly turned and immediately regretted my decision. They looked like such a happy family. Tanner laughing in front of them as Bentley and Staci walked in holding each other's hands. I turned back to face Katie, suddenly not feeling well at all.

"Ireland, are you OK? You're white as a ghost."

"No, I think I'm going to be sick," I said, stuffing the

ultrasound photo back in my purse before running to the restroom.

I splashed some water on my face and took a few calming breaths before walking back out into the restaurant. Just when I thought my day couldn't get any worse, I spotted Bentley at the table talking with my best friend. I momentarily scanned the room for an exit, but sighed in defeat when I realized we were seated next to the only door.

"Hi Ireland," Bentley said hesitantly as I approached the table.

"Hi," I said, giving him a small wave before sitting down in my chair.

"I'm surprised to run into you on this side of the city," Bentley said, trying to make small talk.

"Do you remember where I live," I asked, cautiously.

"No, Greg filled me in a bit."

"Oh. Yeah, well I was just at a doctor's appointment. Katie was craving some pasta so we stopped for lunch."

"Oh, I hope everything's OK."

"Yeah, just a routine appointment. Everything's great," I said, eyeing Katie to make sure she wouldn't let anything slip about the pregnancy. I wasn't ready to deal with everything today—especially with Staci and Tanner sitting less than ten feet away from us.

Just then our waitress walked over with Katie's plate of pasta. "Aren't you eating?" Bentley questioned.

"She's not feeling well," Katie blurted out.

"I thought you just said you were feeling fine," Bentley questioned, furrowing his brow.

"I am. She just meant I'm full. I ate a big breakfast," I said, trying to cover her blunder.

"Oh OK," he said, skeptically.

"How are you doing?" I asked, quickly changing the topic away from me.

"Pretty good. My doctor should be clearing me to go back to work next week. I finally have limited use of my hand," he explained, waving his fingers. "It'll probably take some time for Greg to catch me up on all the accounts, but I need to get back to the grind. Staying cooped up inside all the time is torture."

"Yeah, I bet."

"How's work? Greg told me that you're a counselor?"

Bentley really didn't remember anything about me. I swallowed back the lump in my throat before answering, "Um, yeah. I work mainly with orphans," I said, as Staci walked over to us, slinking her arms around Bentley.

"Jamie, baby, our table is ready," she cooed in his ear, not even paying any attention to me.

"Ok, baby, I'll be right there."

"Tanner is getting hungry. We probably shouldn't keep him waiting."

"Yeah, OK," he said. "Wait, you'd think I'd forgotten my manners in the accident too. Ireland this is Staci and Tanner, my wife and son. This is Ireland. She's an old family friend."

"We've met," Staci said, dangling her hand in front of my face. I couldn't help but notice the huge diamond that was once again secured on her ring finger. Tanner gave me a small wave from behind his mother.

"Right, I should've known," he said, shaking his head.

"It's OK," I said weakly.

"All right, well we'll let you two enjoy the rest of your lunch. Ireland, we should catch up sometime. Maybe grab a coffee?"

"Coffee?" I muttered, lowering my head so he couldn't see the fresh tears that were forming in my eyes. Flashes of our first date playing in my mind. *Parallel parking, Bentley's corny pickup lines, ruby slippers . . .*

"I'm sorry. Was it something I said?" Bentley said, gently placing his hand on the back of my shoulder.

"No." It was all I was able to squeak out before Staci

interjected once again.

"Jamie. We're making this poor hostess wait for us," she whined.

"OK, I'm coming," he told her, before turning to face me once again. "Seriously, Ireland. Call me sometime. I'd love to catch up," he said, pulling a business card from his wallet and handing it to me.

"OK," I said, fingering the card as he turned to walk away.

Just as we were paying our bill, Staci returned to our table.

"Oh hey, look it's the bitch," Katie said. "We don't want to hear what you have to say, Staci, so you can just turn and walk away."

"Trust me, I don't want to make small talk with either of you either," she sneered. "I just came to give Ireland a little warning. You better rip up that business card—or else."

"Or else what, Staci?" Katie chuckled.

"Just don't call him. He's happy. We're happy. Just leave it be," she said, swiveling back around.

"I can't believe I'm admitting this, but I think Staci is right. He's happy. I need to let it go," I said, standing up from the chair.

"You have to tell him about the baby, Ireland," Katie whisper-yelled across the table.

"Shhh. Keep your voice down," I said, ripping up the business card and throwing it on the table.

"I might take you a little more seriously, if I didn't know his digits were permanently stored in your mind."

Rolling my eyes at her, I said, "Can we just leave, please. I need to go home and take a nap. I'm so tired."

"No, you're not getting out of this so easily. I'm serious, Ireland. Bentley needs to know the truth! You know he's going to be devastated when he finds out!"

"Please, just drop it, Katie. I don't want Bentley to come back to me just because he thinks it's the right thing to do. Staci tricked him into marrying her and that's the last thing I want.

I want Bentley to be with me because he loves me and remembers what we share. Not because he feels forced into it."

"I get it. I really do," Katie said, sympathetically. "But, the man deserves to know he's going to be a dad again. He should be able to experience this with you."

"Just let me do this my way!"

Biting her lip, she responded, "I told Greg."

"You did what? Why would you betray me like that, Katie? I trusted you!"

"He's my husband, Ireland. We don't keep secrets from each other. He knew something was bothering me, and I couldn't keep lying to him. You'll understand some day."

She was right. I couldn't hold this against her. I couldn't make her choose between her husband and me. "I'm sorry for getting upset. It's not fair for me to be mad at you."

"Thank you," she said with a slight smile.

"Is he going to tell Bentley?"

"He feels the same way I do. But he'll wait for you to tell him. Neither one of us are going to wait forever though, Ireland. If you don't tell him soon then we eventually will."

"I'll tell him."

"When? You know he's still sitting right over there?"

"Not today. I'll do it soon. Now I'm done with this lecture. I'm exhausted and would like to go home—please."

"Fine, I remember how exhausting the first trimester was. Now I just crave sex—like all the time," she said, rubbing her belly.

"Oh my god," I laughed. "Just take me home."

"What? It's true," she shrugged.

Chapter Seventeen

TANNER AND I had just picked up a steaming pepperoni pizza from Vince's and were heading back to my place for a weekend of male bonding—also known as a weekend filled with playing as many video games as humanly possible.

"Dad, what's this?" Tanner asked, reaching between the SUV's seat to pull out a platinum chain with an attached pendant. The chain was knotted several times as if it'd been crushed between the cushions for several weeks. Tanner hesitated before opening the tiny heart locket.

"There are two pictures of you and Ireland inside," he told me, sadness in his voice.

I wasn't sure why but with just the mention of her name, I felt my heart skip a beat. I hadn't seen her, or talked to her in weeks. Not since that day she'd left me with my wife and son in the restaurant.

"She must have left it in here, huh Dad. Do you think we should take it to her?" Tanner asked.

"I don't think Ireland wants to see me, Son," I said, pulling the Range Rover into the garage and putting it into park.

"Do you think she misses us?" his question surprised me.

I didn't really have an answer for him. We hadn't really talked about my relationship with Ireland—the one I remember nothing about. I guess I'd never really thought about the time that Tanner had probably spent with her.

"Did you like Ireland, buddy?"

"Yeah, I mean she's not my mom, but she was cool to hang out with. I really gave her a hard time at first, but then she kicked both of our asses at Madden."

I chuckled, "That doesn't surprise me. She did learn from the best, you know."

"I know," he said with a smile. "You both told me all about it. I wish you could remember."

"I wish I could remember, too," I said with a touch of melancholy in my voice.

"Dad, I've got something to tell you. I hope you aren't mad at me."

"You know you can tell me anything, Son."

"I should've told you more about how much Ireland meant to you after you woke up. I just wanted you and Mom back together so bad. I really did like Ireland, but I missed our family. I wanted everything to be the way it used to be."

"It's not your fault, Tanner. Your not telling me had nothing to do with my memory coming back. I wanted to try and make things work with your mother, too. Turns out, it's just not meant to be with us. I know that must be hard for you to understand," I said, patting him on the shoulder. "Why don't we go inside and eat this pizza before it gets cold?"

"I think I knew you and Mom wouldn't work though," he practically cried. "I should have told you. I just should have told you!"

"Tanner, was it something specific you should've told me?"

"You loved her so much, Dad. You wanted to marry her. You wanted Ireland to your wife," he yelled. "The weekend before your accident, you sat me down and we had a serious talk. You asked me if it was OK with me if you married Ireland. I told you it was OK, Dad."

"Things were different then, buddy. I know you didn't mean any harm by it."

"You asked me to be your best man, Dad. I didn't act the way a best man should have acted," he sighed, handing me the locket he'd been clutching in his palm. "I let you down. I let Ireland down. You told me you loved her, Dad. And, I know she loved you, too."

I opened the locket and on the right was a picture of the two of us in one of those photo booths. She was wearing a wine-colored gown and I was in a matching vest and white button-down shirt. From our wardrobe, I could only assume we'd been at Greg and Katie's wedding. Greg told me that's where I'd run into Ireland again.

I felt terrible telling my best friend and business partner that I didn't remember anything about his wedding, but sadly it was true. All I knew about the last year of my life was what people had tried telling me—hoping that I would remember for myself. But, even after all of the stories, I was coming up blank. Suddenly, in a flicker, I saw myself in what looked like a movie reel playing out in slow motion.

I was in the middle of a conversation with Katie's brother, Tim, when I saw Katie come out of her bridal suite with a gorgeous blonde wearing a strapless wine-colored dress. Our eyes locked and she took my breath away. I knew her from somewhere. I just couldn't place it. The sudden expression on her face made me think that she knew me too.

She was intoxicating and I had to know who she was—how she fit into my life. Excusing myself from Tim, I walked toward Katie and the mysterious bridesmaid. She looked very rattled and I wanted to make sure everything was all set for the wedding. After all, I think those are the duties of the best man.

"Is everything all right over here?" I asked, walking toward the two women. "Katie, my best friend sure is one lucky man. You look

beautiful."

"Thank you, Jamie," she said, wrapping her arms around my shoulders and pulling me in for warm embrace and gentle kiss on the cheek. I'd always had a soft spot for my best friend's soon-to-be wife. The next words out of her mouth shocked me. She could've told me that aliens would soon invade planet Earth and turn us all into sea creatures within five minutes, and I wouldn't have been more shocked.

"Jamie, this is my best friend and maid of honor—Ireland." There is no way she just said her best friend's name was Ireland. It's not a common name. Not at all. Am I breathing? I'm not sure I'm breathing.

Say something you idiot. She probably thinks you're crazy just staring at her. "Ireland? That's a pretty uncommon name?"

"Dad? Are you OK? You don't look so hot," I heard Tanner ask from beside me.

"Uh huh," I mumbled. "Take the pizza inside. I'll be there in a minute."

Tanner grabbed the pizza from the backseat and stepped out of the vehicle. I watched as he walked into the house before glancing at the picture on the left. It was a selfie of the two of us wrapped in a blanket lying on the floor of my folks' cabin in Tennessee. Ireland had gone back to Tennessee with me?

"Ahhhhhhhh," I screamed. "Why is this happening to me? Why can't I remember. Just let me remember."

Another flicker . . .

I was in the guestroom of the cabin, getting myself more comfortable before slipping into bed. I'd offered to stay on the couch for the night, but Ireland insisted on me coming back to the bedroom with her. Although I'd talked a big game, I didn't intend on rushing anything between us. If I'm being honest, I just enjoyed watching her face flush and her hands fidget when I said something inappropriate. She acted shy, but knew how to play the game well herself. After a few feisty comments, I wanted to get down on my hands and knees and beg her to fuck me.

The door creaking open alerted me that Ireland had joined me in the room. I quickly closed the drawer of the nightstand, turned and looked up to see Ireland standing there only wearing a light pink, sheer nightie. Her tits filled out the top perfectly. Just the sight of her gave me an instant hard-on. I reached down and readjusted myself, fearful I would shoot my load before I'd even touched her.

I sauntered toward her—wanting to eliminate the space between us. We met at the edge of the bed, but I stopped her just before she reached me.

"Stop right there," I growled. "I need to look at you."

I felt bad devouring her with my eyes. I didn't want to make her uncomfortable, but at the same time I needed to see all of her.

"This is a first for me," she said, breaking the silence in the room. "I've never made love before."

At first, I didn't understand exactly what she was saying. As much as I wished I would be her first and her last, I knew that it couldn't possibly be the case.

"You're not making any sense, Shamrock. I know you can't possibly be a virgin," I said with a shake of my head.

She laughed softly before responding, "No, I'm definitely not a virgin. I don't think you understand what I'm saying . . . I've had sex before, but I've not made love before."

Realization struck me. Ireland loved me. I needed her to know that I loved her too. I think a part of me always had loved her.

I swallowed, my nerves getting the best of me, "Are you saying what I think you're saying, Ireland? Do you love me?"

Wait. What are you asking her? You can't make her say it first. What man makes the love of his life say those three words before she hears him say them first?

"I–." she started. I stopped her, pulling her forward so only inches separated us, placing a single finger against her lips.

Here goes nothing. "Because I love you, Ireland."

My words brought tears to her eyes. I reached out and touched her cheek, catching a falling drop with the pad of my thumb.

"Don't cry, Shamrock. You don't have to say anything. I just *wanted you to know how I was feeling."* Although I said the words, I was secretly saying a silent prayer that she would say the words. And, yes, it's quite possible that in just a short span of five minutes, I, James Bentley Roberts had grown a vagina.

"I do, Bentley. I love you, too," she whispered. Sweet music to my ears.

I whipped my cell from my pocket and shot a quick text off to Tanner. I needed to go see Ireland. I couldn't let any more time go to waste.

Dad: I have a quick errand I need to run. Will you be OK for a little while on your own?

Tanner: I'll be fine, Dad. I'm practically fourteen. And, that's practically an adult, you know.

Dad: Ha! You've got a few years until you're an adult. Don't go outside and don't let anyone in the house. I'll be back as soon as I can.

Tanner: I got it Dad! News flash: I'm not a kid anymore. Mom lets me stay at her house alone all the time.

Dad: Don't get snarky with me, son. But, I trust you so I'll see you when I get home. Save me some pizza and you can show me those new video games you were telling me about.

Tanner: Sure, Dad. But, I can't make any promises about the pizza.

Like father like son, I thought to myself. I set my phone and Ireland's locket down in the seat next to me before backing out of the driveway. I was going to reclaim my girl. I was asking her to marry me—tonight. I just hoped that too much time hadn't already passed.

Chapter Eighteen

I'D JUST PULLED a piping hot pizza out of the oven and was sitting down to catch up on my DVR recordings when there was a rap on my door.

Looking down at my cell, I saw it was approaching nine o'clock. *Who could be knocking at my door at this hour?* Standing up, I felt my baby wiggle inside my belly. I was nearing my twentieth week of pregnancy and the little bugger had been quite active in the last few weeks. At first, I thought I was experiencing indigestion from all of the taco salads I'd been craving. But, after several hours and some internet research, I realized it was actually my Little Bean—the nickname I'd given my baby when I first saw him or her swimming around on the screen during my initial ultrasound.

I rubbed my now protruding baby bump, which was barely concealed under my oversized sweatshirt, as I padded to the front door. Looking out the peephole, I was stunned to see Bentley standing on the other side of the door. I thought about not answering, but he'd clearly seen my car which was parked in the driveway. If I let him in, he'd see that I was pregnant and he'd have so many questions. My mind began to swirl and I was beginning to feel lightheaded.

"Ireland, I know you're inside. Please open the door. We really need to talk."

Did Katie tell him about the baby? I was seriously going to kill my best friend. I'd be a pregnant woman in jail because I would be put away for murder. I hoped Greg was ready to be a single father. Or, maybe it was actually Greg. Maybe I'd have to murder him just to be safe. Oh my god, now I'm acting like an axe-wielding, crazy person. Blame it on the pregnancy hormones. There was no other excuse for thinking it would be OK to kill your best friend and her husband.

"Shamrock, please," Bentley said once again.

Wait, did he just call me Shamrock? That's odd.

I took a deep breath before slowly opening the door.

We stared at each other for a moment before Bentley spoke. "Tanner found this between the seats of the SUV," he said, holding out the locket he'd given me months before. He'd surprised me with it as an early birthday present after we'd gone to the recreation center with the kids. The fact that he'd combined a piece of our past with our present made my heart melt.

"I see," I said, nodding in understanding. "You came by because you thought I'd want it back?"

"Well, yes, but there's more, Ireland," he started to explain.

"It's OK, Bentley. You don't need to explain. You can keep the locket if you'd like. It doesn't mean anything to me anymore anyways," I said as I began to shut the door on him.

"Ireland, stop!" he shouted, putting his hand against the door. "You need to listen to me. I did think you'd want the locket. It meant so much to you when I gave it to you when we were sitting outside the putt-putt course waiting for the kids to finish. I remember the sadness in your eyes when you'd thought it was lost."

It took me a minute to absorb Bentley's words. "How—how did you know we were sitting outside the putt-putt course? I never told anyone that and I didn't think anyone had seen us," I said with confusion in my voice.

"I remember," he said softly.

"You remember? What do you remember?" I asked, tears now beginning to stream down my face.

"I remember everything, Shamrock. I remember the wedding, the coffeehouse, the cabin, the dinners, the breakfasts—and definitely what came between the dinners and breakfasts," he said with a wink. "Most importantly, I remember you, Ireland."

Bentley took the pad of his thumb to wipe the corner of my eye. "You remember me?" I asked, hesitantly.

"I remember you. All of you. I love you, Ireland Erin O'Brien," he said, pulling me closer to him to capture my lips with his own.

"What about Staci," I asked, pulling away.

"I haven't been with her in two months. Even though I couldn't remember everything, I knew something wasn't right between us. I moved back to my place. I've been wanting to come see you, but I didn't want things to be awkward between us," he explained. "I'm so sorry, Shamrock. Please tell me we can start over."

"Bentley, I—I have something to tell you."

Something caught Bentley's eye; he began looking me up and down. "I think I have a pretty good idea what you're going to tell me," he said, his voice filled with anger. "Are you pregnant, Ireland?"

I stared at him blankly, my head beginning to pound.

"Answer the goddamned question, Ireland. Are you fucking pregnant?"

"Yes," I muttered, barely audible even to my own ears.

"Is it even my baby?" he sneered.

Now it was my turn to get angry. I knew I'd hurt him, but he'd drawn the line by asking if it was his baby.

"Of course it's your baby!" I screamed. "What kind of fucking question is that, Bentley?"

"A pretty fucking obvious one, I think. We haven't been

together for months. How would I know who you're fucking? You didn't think it was necessary to tell me about it, so it would make sense if it was someone else's."

"Well it's not," I cried, smacking him in the chest. "It's yours. I haven't been with anyone but you since the day I ran into you again at Katie's wedding!"

He took a deep breath, calming himself slightly, before he asked his next question. "OK, so you're carrying my baby. I still don't understand why you didn't tell me. Please help me make sense of this!"

"I did tell you, or at least I tried to tell you," I sobbed.

"I don't remember your telling me, Ireland. I thought all my memories were back, but I don't remember your telling me you were pregnant with my child. I'm pretty sure I would remember something as significant as that."

"You were unconscious," I whispered.

He chuckled before responding, "I see. So you thought telling me I was going to be a father again while I was unconscious was good enough? Didn't you think I deserved to know the truth, Ireland? Were you ever going to tell me when I was conscious? Or did you just plan on sending me a Father's Day card in five years—congratulations, you're a daddy!"

"I was going to tell you. I swear, I was going to tell you."

"When Ireland? When were you going to tell me? From the looks of things, this isn't something you just found out!"

"I found out right after the accident. You were in the hospital. I was constantly throwing up. I assumed it was just nerves, but when it didn't go away I bought a pregnancy test from the hospital gift shop. I took it in the bathroom and immediately came out and told you. Then you woke up and didn't remember me. What was I supposed to say, Bentley? Hi, I'm Ireland. You loved me when we were kids and we found our way back to each other in the last six months. You were going to marry me. Oh, and by the way, I'm having your baby? You see, that may have worked except there was one other hitch . . . you thought you were still married to your ex-fucking-wife!"

Bentley just stared at me, not saying a word.

"Now you have nothing to say?" I asked.

"I know it was hard for you, Ireland. But, I still deserved to know."

"You're right. You did. But, I didn't want you back just because I was pregnant. You would have stayed with me just like you stayed with Staci when she got pregnant with Tanner. You told me how much you regretted that decision. I didn't want you to regret me. So, it was better to just walk away. Maybe it was the wrong decision, but it was my decision to make."

"I guess I understand. I don't agree, but I understand," he said, turning to walk back down the sidewalk.

"Where are you going?" I asked.

"I'm not sure. I need some time to think."

"I really am sorry, Bentley."

He reached the end of the sidewalk and turned on his heels once again. "Is it a boy or a girl?" he questioned.

"I'm not sure yet. I'm planning on finding out next week." I contemplated inviting him to the appointment, but feared his rejection too much to say the words.

He nodded before sliding into the Range Rover. I watched him back down the driveway before closing the door and bursting into uncontrollable tears.

About forty-five minutes later, I was still on the floor sobbing when my phone rang. I said a silent prayer that it was Bentley. "Hello," I said, trying to hide the trembling in my voice.

"Oh my god, Ireland," Katie nearly screamed. "Are you OK? Bentley just left here. He stopped by pretty shaken up. He's furious with Greg and me for not telling him your secret."

"I'm so sorry. I regret having involved you two. I should've told Bentley just liked you said. I'll understand if you never want to speak to me again."

"Ireland, you're my best friend. You're practically my sister. I may not have agreed with your decision, but I told you I would go along with it. I made the decision to back you just as you made the decision that you felt was best for you and your baby."

"But, I've made things uncomfortable for Greg too. He's Bentley's best friend. He sees him every day at work. I'm so sorry. Please tell him how sorry I am."

"We both know, sweetie. You need to calm down for the baby's sake. Do you need me to come over?"

"No, you have a newborn there who needs his mommy more than I do. I'll be fine, I promise. I'm just going to try and get some sleep anyways. All I want to do is stay in bed for the next four to five months. Give Shawn big smooches from his auntie," I said, before ending the call.

Grabbing a pillow off the couch, I rested my head against it. I must have been so emotionally drained after Bentley's visit that I soon succumbed to sleep. Waking up several hours later, my every joint was aching from head to toe from sleeping on the floor. I managed to pry myself off the carpet and padded to the bedroom where I crawled into bed and stayed for the next two days.

Chapter Nineteen

GETTING READY FOR my doctor's appointment, I heard my phone bing with an incoming text. I grabbed it off my dresser, hoping that it was Bentley saying that he'd go to the appointment with me. I was finding out the baby's gender and I really wanted him to be a part of it. He'd already missed so much and the only person to blame for that was me.

> *Katie: Isn't your appointment this afternoon? Want me to go with you? I can see if Greg's mom wants to watch Shawn for a bit.*

I loved Katie so much and really didn't know what I would do without her. But, I'd been leaning on her too much lately and needed to start learning how to deal with everything on my own again. I'd done it once before; I could do it again.

> *Ireland: No, I'm good. Thank you for always thinking of me though. This is something I need to do alone though. I did send the information to Bentley, but he never responded. I'm guessing he doesn't want anything to do with me. Hopefully he'll eventually come around for the baby's sake.*

> *Katie: You know he's a good man, Ireland. You know as well as I do that Bentley will be there for this child just like he's been there*

for Tanner all these years. Lord knows, Staci hasn't made it easy for him.

Ireland: I know. I just really thought I would've heard from him by now. I need to finish getting ready now. I'll text you after the appointment and let you know how it goes.

Katie: Eeeeep! I can't wait to hear if I'm going to have a little niece or nephew to spoil!

I rushed into the doctor's office with only minutes to spare. Parking had been a nightmare—with only parallel parking available. I had to park in a city lot about a half-mile away from the health center. Although it was a relatively cool, early summer day, I was sweating and out of breath when I walked up to the receptionist's counter.

"Hi there," I said as she opened the sliding glass window to greet me. "I hope I'm not late. I'm Ireland O'Brien. I'm here for my appointment with Dr. Rhoads."

"Yes, Miss O'Brien. You're right on time and the doctor is running a little behind anyways. Not to worry, you've already been checked in. You may have a seat and we'll call you back when the doctor is ready to see you."

"I don't understand," I said, confusedly. "Who could've checked me in?"

"I'm sorry. That gentleman sitting in the corner checked you in," she said, pointing toward the opposite side of the room. Being so flustered when I walked into the office, I hadn't even noticed anyone sitting in the waiting room. "He said he was with you. I just assumed he was the baby's father."

As I turned to look, I'm fairly certain my heart stopped momentarily. Bentley was sitting in one of the chairs with his elbows resting on his knees, raking his hair with his fingers. He looked terrible. I mean as terrible as Bentley could ever look.

Sure, he was still handsome as ever, but he looked defeated. It appeared as if he hadn't slept in days. I felt a sudden pang in my chest, realizing what I'd put him through.

"Miss, are you OK. Have I overstepped?" the receptionist asked.

"No, no. It's fine. He's my baby's father. Thank you," I re-assured her, giving her a forced smile as I turned and walked toward Bentley.

"Hi," I said, biting the inside of my cheek. "I didn't expect to see you here. You never returned my messages."

He looked up and stared at me in silence for several seconds before answering, "I wasn't sure if I was coming. I guess you could say it was a last minute decision, but here I am."

"Well, I'm glad you decided to come," I said in a tired voice.

"I didn't do it for you, Ireland. I did it for our child. No matter what happens between us, I will always be there for my son or daughter."

"OK," I muttered, lowering my head so he wouldn't see my tears.

We waited in silence for several minutes before a nurse opened the door into the exam area and called my name. Rising from my seat, I began walking toward the nurse before realizing Bentley hadn't gotten up yet,

I turned to face him, before asking, "Well, are you coming?"

"Yeah, I just didn't know if you wanted me in the room for everything. I thought maybe someone could just come and call for me when they were doing the ultrasound."

"Don't be ridiculous, Bentley. You've seen me naked. We can both be adults about this."

"Fine," he said as he stood and followed me into the office.

I changed into the paper gown laid out for me on the exam table as Bentley took a seat in one of the chairs across the room. The nurse charted my vitals before Dr. Rhoads entered and greeted both Bentley and me.

"Ireland, it's nice to see you again. How have you been feeling since your last visit?" she asked.

"It's nice to see you again, too, Dr. Rhoads. I've been feeling pretty good actually. Those pills you prescribed for the nausea have helped tremendously. Maybe too well, actually. The nurse said I'd gained almost twelve pounds since my appointment last month."

"Normally, I would tell you to watch your calorie intake after seeing that kind of rapid weight gain, but since you actually lost weight during your first trimester, I don't as yet see a problem. But, to be on the safe side, I think I'll order you a blood glucose test. Typically, we'd wait until you were a bit further along, but I don't think it'll hurt to go ahead and do it now just to check things out," she explained, turning toward Bentley. "And, I assume this is the baby's father?"

"Yes, I'm James Roberts," he said, shaking Dr. Rhoads' hand. "It's nice to meet you, Dr. Rhoads. I'm sorry I was—unavailable—for Ireland's other appointments."

After checking my heartbeat and examining my belly for any abnormalities, Dr. Rhoads removed a blood pressure cuff from the equipment drawer.

"I know the nurse already took your blood pressure while she was checking your vitals, but I'd like to measure it again," she explained. "It was quite high, and if I'm being honest I'm concerned."

I didn't want to worry, but I'd read about high blood pressure during pregnancy and I feared complications such as preeclampsia and placental abruption.

"Is everything OK," I asked, as the blood pressure cuff squeezed my arm tighter and tighter.

"It's come down a bit from when you first got here, but it's still about 140/90 which causes some concern. Ireland, have you had any extra stress in your life since your last visit," she asked, pointedly.

"I suppose you could say that," I said, glancing toward Bentley, fidgeting in his chair.

"Well, I don't want to intrude in your personal business, but as your healthcare provider, I suggest you work things out, if at all possible—for your welfare and your baby's."

"I'll do my best," I said.

"I'm serious, Ireland. I'd like you to schedule an appointment again in another two weeks so we can see that it's come down. If it hasn't, I'll have to put you on permanent bed rest. Now enough of the lecture, let's get you prepped for your ultrasound. Are you ready to find out what you're having?"

"Yes, I've been looking forward to this moment since I last saw the Little Bean," I said with a smile.

"Little Bean?" Bentley questioned, as he got up from his seat and walked toward me.

"Yeah, when Dr. Rhoads did my first ultrasound, the baby was the size of a bean and the name kind of stuck. I've been calling it Little Bean ever since," I shrugged.

Pulling my gown up above my belly, Dr. Rhoads squirted the cold gel on my bump. She placed the transducer on my skin and a fuzzy image immediately appeared.

"There's your baby," Dr. Rhoads said, pointing toward the screen to show Bentley. "It's a little bigger than a bean now, Ireland."

"What's that whooshing sound," Bentley asked with a look of adoration on his face. It was the first time I'd seen his smile in weeks and the sight made my heart begin to soar.

"That's your baby's heartbeat. It's coming in strong and steady today at 145 beats per minute."

"Is that normal. Is everything OK," Bentley asked, with concern in his voice. "It's been so long since my son was born. I forget the details."

"Yes, everything is fine. Everything appears perfect, actually," she said, smiling. "Would you like to know the gender now, or are you having one of those reveal parties that have become so popular these days? I can write it in an envelope for you if you'd prefer."

"No, no party. You can just tell us now," I answered.

"OK, well the fetus has actually given me a perfect view so I can say with one hundred percent certainty that you're having a girl."

"A baby girl," I said, as tears formed in my eyes. In that moment, I felt my mom's presence in the room. She would have loved a granddaughter and I know she would have spoiled her rotten.

"We're having a little girl," Bentley said, reaching to squeeze my hand. It was the first time he'd touched me since he'd learned the truth. I wasn't going to assume that he'd forgiven me, but, in that moment, I was hopeful that things would be OK.

Bentley stayed in the room for a few minutes as I was dressing.

"Like I told you earlier, Ireland, I want nothing more than to be a father to our daughter. I've only seen her once, but I know I love her already," Bentley said.

"You know you can always be a part of her life. She will always need her daddy," I whispered.

"I want to be a part of your life, too, but I don't know in what capacity," he said. "The fact that you kept this secret from me for so long has really hurt. I'm not sure I can trust you again. But, I'm trying to understand."

"Thank you," I said, quietly. "I really am sorry. I know I don't deserve your forgiveness, but I really am sorry."

Just then, Dr. Rhoads knocked and opened the door. She was carrying the orders for the glucose test and other various bloodwork.

"I just wanted to see that you got these. I also wanted to let you know about some upcoming birthing classes that the hospital will be offering on Saturdays starting in about three weeks. I hope that you both sign up. I think they're very educational and informative sessions and I encourage all of my parents-to-be to take them."

I CALLED KATIE the minute I'd left the doctor's office. She must have been holding her phone in anticipation because she picked up on the first ring.

"So, am I having a niece or a nephew. Please tell me a niece because I bought the most adorable pink dresses and bows and Greg would murder me if I tried dressing Shawn in them," she said, without even a hello.

"It's a girl!" I shrieked into the phone.

"Ahhhhhhhhh," she screamed. "Our babies really are going to get married!"

"Will you stop it with that! Our babies will probably end up hating each other."

"Oh my god. You didn't just say that! Take it back! Ireland Erin O'Brien, you take it back right now, or I'm ending this call."

"OK, OK. I take it back. Our babies will love and adore one another and give us beautiful grandbabies someday," I laughed.

"OK, you took that too far. My baby boy is never having sex."

"You're ridiculous," I chuckled.

"So, did Bentley show up for the appointment?"

"Yeah," I said, nodding my head even though she couldn't see.

"He really did? I bet that was super awkward. How did it go?"

I let out a long sigh before answering, "I mean I guess it went as well as could be expected. He wants to be a part of our daughter's life, but he's not sure he can ever trust me again. I think it's really over between us."

"You don't know that, Ireland. He'll come around."

"I wish I could say you're right, but I really don't think so this time."

Chapter Twenty

AS I WAS finishing up my morning paperwork, Katie barged into my office unannounced.

"I was in the area and I'm starving," she said. "Want to go grab a bite to eat with me?"

"You know what a phone is, right?" I asked.

"Yeah, why?"

"Because I really wish you would've used it. I've had a killer headache all morning and I'm trying to get my paperwork finished so I can go home for the rest of the day."

Before I'd finished my rant, Katie spotted the almost-empty bottle of Tylenol on my desk.

"You should be careful with those," she warned.

"Thank you, Mother—I know. Dr. Rhoads said they'd be OK to take. I'm not an idiot."

"In moderation," she shouted. "This bottle is practically empty. These aren't candy, Ireland. This can't be good for the baby."

"I only took two today. Would you relax?

"Today? How often are you having these headaches?"

"Seems like recently, I've had one every day. I just figured it was a side effect from the pregnancy."

"Have you told the doctor?"

"No, I have an appointment next week and was going to tell

her then. I'm sure it's nothing."

"Didn't you tell me that you were dizzy the other night, too?" she asked.

"Yeah, why? It just happened once. It's not a big deal."

"Ireland, if you don't call Dr. Rhoads right now, then I will. This is more than nothing. And, it's definitely a big deal. You shouldn't be relying on Tylenol to get you through every day."

"Fine," I huffed, picking up my phone to dial the doctor.

Following the doctor's orders, Katie took me directly to the ER. I was poked, prodded and hooked up to every monitor imaginable within a matter of minutes.

"I told you this was more than nothing," Katie said, sternly.

"Fine. You're right. I'm worried I should've called the doctor sooner. What if I hurt the baby?" I said with concern in my voice.

Just then, Dr. Rhoads came into the room.

"Ireland, I would say it's good to see you. But, I don't really enjoy seeing my patients under these circumstances," she said, grabbing my chart from the door. "You did the right thing by calling me. Just as I feared, your blood pressure has spiked. It was 160/110 when you came in. I think I'm going to admit you for observation. I'm not comfortable sending you home while it's still that high."

"Is the baby OK?"

"The baby's heart rate was strong and everything appears to check out. I'll order an ultrasound once you get settled in your room."

ONCE I'D GOTTEN settled, I was completely worn out and exhausted. Katie said she'd go down to the cafeteria for a bit while I tried to get some sleep. For nearly forty-five minutes I tried to fall asleep, but a hospital was hardly the best place to catch up on sleep. I laughed, thinking that my blood pressure would have a better chance of dropping if I'd checked into the Hilton.

I tried calling Bentley several times from the hospital, but he hadn't picked up. Finally leaving a message, I explained the situation. I didn't think he'd actually come up to see me so I was a bit surprised when I heard him talking to Katie out in the hallway.

"I don't think you should go in there," Katie said.

"Why not?" He asked, sounding exasperated.

"Because you'll just upset her! Don't you get it! You're the reason she's in here in the first place. She's been so stressed out worrying about your relationship, or lack thereof, that she hasn't been taking care of herself. She's not eating. She's not sleeping. She's barely functioning," Katie whisper-yelled.

"I think I need to talk to her," he said desperately.

"I just don't think it's a good idea right now, Bentley. Her doctor said she needs to remove all the stresses from her life before the baby's born. She won't be working for a few months now, either. I'll tell her you were here. Just please go," Katie begged.

I wasn't initially happy at what Katie had done, but I understood why she did it. Talking with Bentley would only upset me further and that was the last thing I needed right now. After a few more hours of watching pointless, reality television, I finally drifted off to sleep.

After spending two days in the hospital, Dr. Rhoads allowed me to go home. I was ordered to stay on bed rest for at least a week, and wouldn't be going back to work until after the baby was born. I was sure it wasn't the stress of work causing my anxiety, but I wasn't comfortable sharing the details of my personal life with my obstetrician so I agreed to it.

TRYING TO OBEY the doctor's orders, I lay in bed catching up on the latest season of *The Bachelor*. Just then I received an unexpected text message. I stared at his name on the screen, hesitating for a moment before opening it. After all, I'd finally been able to get my anxiety and blood pressure under control and the last thing I needed was to wind up back in the hospital—especially when Dr. Rhoads had warned me that the next time might be for the duration of my pregnancy.

I took a deep breath, calming my nerves, as I slid my finger across the screen, opening the message.

> *Bentley: Greg told me that you'd been released from the hospital. I'm not sure how much Katie told you, but I tried visiting you while you were there. She thought it'd be best if I stayed away for a while. It pains me to say it, but I think she was right. Anyways, I think I'm rambling now. I just wanted you to know that I've been thinking about you constantly.*

> *Ireland: I did hear that you stopped by to see me. Thank you for caring. I wish things didn't have to be this way between us. If only we could travel back in time, and change some of the decisions that we made.*

> *Bentley: As much as I don't show it sometimes, I'll always care about you, Shamrock. But, I know you need your rest so I'll stop bothering you.*

> *Ireland: It's OK. I'm actually wide awake and there are only so many episodes of The Bachelor I can watch before I start going crazy. As much as the thought of staying in bed all day sounds fantastic, it's really not all it's cracked up to be.*

> *Bentley: LOL I can see that. Too bad I'm not there. I'm sure we could find a way to make use of our time.*

I reread Bentley's message a few times to make sure I wasn't seeing things. Was he actually flirting with me? Before I had too much time to think about it, another message appeared.

Bentley: I'm sorry. I shouldn't have said that, I'll let you get back to those bachelor hunks. Do you have any appointments coming up that I might be able to go to?

Ireland: Actually, I've been meaning to message you. I was able to schedule the birthing class. It's next Saturday, and I was hoping maybe you could come with me.

Bentley: I wouldn't miss it. I can swing by and pick you up. That way you won't have to worry about hospital parking.

Ireland: That'd be perfect. It starts at 10 a.m. and I can be ready around 9:30. That should give us plenty of time.

Bentley: I'll see you then. It was good talking to you, Ireland. I really do miss this.

Ireland: Me too.

Bentley: Don't hesitate to call me if you need anything. And, I mean anything.

I smiled, knowing full well what he meant, but thought I could play it to my advantage anyways.

Ireland: So, if I asked you to bring me a pickle and peanut butter sandwich, you would?

Bentley: I don't think I even want to know. But, I did say anything. Where would I find one of those?

Ireland: I'm just kidding. Ish. I'll see you next Saturday.

Bentley: See you then.

ABOUT FIFTEEN COUPLES had taken their places on the floor, pregnant women resting against their partners' backs, waiting in anticipation for the birthing class to begin. Most of the couples were married, some engaged, others—like us—chose not to share their stories.

Our instructor talked about her many experiences as a labor and delivery nurse and about various complications that may arise during childbirth, as well as pain management techniques. We were given the opportunity to chat with the other couples and share our pregnancy stories—primarily those involving late night cravings.

"Cake! All I constantly crave is cake," one of the expectant mothers confessed. "I woke up at three in the morning once and made my husband drive to the nearest 24/7 grocery store to buy me an entire sheet cake. I'm a little embarrassed to admit that I ate the whole thing."

Bentley leaned over and whispered into my ear, "Have you had any other weird cravings—besides the pickle and peanut butter sandwiches of course?"

"Garlic bread sticks with cream cheese," I laughed. "Speaking of which, I think I need those in my life like right now."

"That sounds disgusting," he chuckled. "Although I suppose not as disgusting as your sandwiches."

"Oh my god. Don't knock it until you try it," I said, giving him the evil eye. "But, I'll forgive you since you surprised me with a sandwich for breakfast this morning."

"I'll just take your word for it. Where do you usually go to get those? Because maybe we could have dinner sometime this week?"

"Are—are you asking me out on a date?"

"I already knocked you up, Ireland. A date doesn't seem quite appropriate. But, yes, I guess I'm asking you to have dinner with me."

"I'd love to," I said with a half-smile. I didn't want to read too much into his behavior, but I felt like this was a step in the right direction. Maybe he was only doing this for our daughter's sake, but I had to hope it was more than that.

With only twenty minutes left in the session, the instructor took us through various prenatal and breathing exercises. She showed us various pelvic exercises that were used to alleviate back pain during pregnancy. It was the closest and most intimate the two of us had been in months.

After the class, Bentley took me back to my place. We each sat in the Rover for several minutes joking and catching up. For once it wasn't awkward, but easy and carefree.

"I should probably get going inside. The baby's crib was delivered a few days ago, and Katie and Greg are coming over later to help me assemble it. I still need to tidy up a bit," I explained.

"Would Katie mind if you canceled?" he asked.

"I don't understand. Why would I cancel? It needs to get done, or our baby will be sleeping on the floor and I don't think that's a very safe place for her."

"I just meant that I'd like to come in and help you instead."

"Oh," I said, with surprise in my voice. "Sure, if you want to. I'm sure she wouldn't mind at all."

"OK, let's do this then," he said, getting out of the SUV.

After being so in tune to each other's bodies during the birthing session, I was beyond hot and bothered by the time we'd made it inside. I wasn't sure if it was because I hadn't been physically intimate with anyone in months, or if Bentley really had been sending me all the right signals during the class, and afterwards in the car.

I went to change while Bentley went into the nursery to start assembling the baby's crib. I guess I'd been reading him wrong the entire time. He only wanted to come back to my place so he could help build furniture, not have wild, pregnancy sex.

Although hot summer air had been replaced with a cool autumn breeze, I was still sweltering from being nearly eight months pregnant. I took off my sweater, jeans, and knee-high boots and changed into a pair of athletic shorts and a light camisole before making my way into the baby's nursery.

"I see you found the toolbox OK," I said. "Can I get you anything to drink? I may still have a few beers in the fridge from the last time Greg and Katie were here."

"No, I'm OK for now. Thanks though," he said, as he began unpacking the crib.

"Anything I can do to help?"

"Nah, I got it."

Well this is going great. Talk about awkward conversation. "All right, I guess I'll just go and read for a while then. Holler if you need anything," I said, walking out and heading down the hall.

But before I knew it, Bentley was standing behind me, his arms wrapped around my very round belly.

"Wait, please don't leave," he said, lightly massaging my stomach. Just then, I felt our daughter begin to stir.

"Was that? Did she just move?" he asked.

I giggled, "Yes, that's her. She's going to be a dancer for sure. Always movin' and shakin'."

"That's incredible. Was that her again?"

"Yeah, touch right here. That's where you can feel her the best," I said, placing my hand on top of his."

"I can't believe I've missed so much," he mumbled, turning me around to face him.

"I can't do this anymore, Ireland. I can't be without you—either of you," he said, seizing my lips with a kiss.

I pulled away, needing to distance myself from him. In my head, I wasn't sure if this was the right thing. My body said yes, but this was about more than satisfying a need. I had so much more to think about. It wasn't just about me anymore, it was my baby, too.

I couldn't stand the thought of losing Bentley for a third time. What if something else happened—what if next time I lost him for good? Maybe it was best just to say our goodbyes now before it was too late. He would still be a part of his daughter's life, but I would just go back to the life I lived before Bentley had stormed back into it.

"Ireland, stop it. I know what you're doing. I can see it in your eyes. I'm not letting you pull away from me. Not now."

"It's just—I can't lose you again, Bentley. I've already lost you twice. I can't even bear the thought of losing you for a third time. I think it would literally kill me," I said.

"I'm not going anywhere—not again."

Before I had time to comprehend what was happening between us, Bentley was grazing the underside of my breasts through the thin cotton. I hadn't felt his hands on me for months and I yearned for his touch.

I let go of my fears once and for all and gave into my desires. "Please, Bentley. Touch me," I said, leaning further into him.

Groaning, he moved his fingers to my already pebbled nipples, "I've missed you, Shamrock. I've missed this. God, have I missed this," he said, as he flicked each hardened bud.

I dropped my head back allowing him access to nip and suck on my neck. He began at my clavicle and drew a line of kisses up my neck to the base of my ear.

He blew lightly before whispering, "Are you sure you're comfortable? We can stop if this will hurt you, or the baby?"

"Yes, this is perfectly OK—more than OK, actually."

He reached for my hand and led me to the bedroom. Once inside, he sat me on the edge of the bed before groping for the hem of my camisole, and then pulling it over my shoulders. I lifted my hips so he could slide my shorts and panties down my thighs. He kissed his way back up my body, starting at my thighs and stopping at my center before moving upward toward my navel and breasts.

"You're beautiful, Ireland. You've always been gorgeous in my eyes. But, seeing you nude while carrying my baby—there isn't even a word in the English language to describe the way I'm feeling right now."

He stopped, his eyes almost begging for permission to kiss me. My lips parted and he slipped his tongue inside. Feeling a fire erupt in my core, I begged to be touched.

Kissing me several more times, he stood up to get undressed. I looked up at him with hooded eyes as he began removing his clothing—piece by piece.

As if sensing my urgent need, Bentley lay back down and slowly slid into my already wet and wanting pussy. I gasped at his sudden entrance. I'd forgotten just how well he could satisfy me so completely, making me feel whole.

"I love you, Ireland. I will never let this much time pass again without feeling your walls tighten around my cock. You complete me."

My heart fluttered at his words. "I love you, too, Bentley. Only you. Always you," I moaned.

Bentley began rocking back and forth, skillfully using his fingers to fondle me everywhere. It was almost as if he thought I would vanish into thin air. After the last few months we'd had, along with our history, I could understand and craved his touch as much as he craved mine.

Both of us being on the edge of ecstatic release, Bentley brought two fingers to my clit and began rubbing in a circular motion. I groaned as he began thrusting himself into me, picking up the pace.

"Bentley," I screamed, as my body began writhing beneath

him in utter pleasure.

Just as I felt myself coming down from my own high, he pumped into me once more before erupting inside me. His body went limp as his hard cock continued to twitch inside my walls. After several more minutes, he removed himself from me. Our breathing began to slow and Bentley kissed the corner of my lips.

We lay there for a few minutes, letting our hearts slow to a normal pace. Bentley was the first to speak, "Have you thought about baby names?"

I smiled at his question. "Actually, I've marked off a few in a book of names."

"What are they?"

"McKenna."

"It's OK. What else?"

"Glenda."

"Really? *Wizard of Oz* again?"

"No. That was Glinda," I laughed.

"Close enough. Any others?"

"Yeah, but if you hate it then I'm going to cry."

"Tell me," he encouraged.

"Lexi."

"That's it!" he exclaimed. "Lexi Lynn Roberts?"

"How did you know I wanted her middle name to be Lynn?" I questioned.

"Because it was your mother's name and I wouldn't have it any other way," he said, pulling me into a warm embrace.

Before I had a chance to respond to the choice of names, Bentley got up and began rummaging through his clothes before slipping on a pair of jeans. Sadness washed over me as I realized our little reunion was only temporary.

"Are you leaving?" I asked, wrapping myself in the sheet.

"No, I'm not going anywhere," he said, kneeling beside the bed.

"What are you doing then?" I asked, a bit confused.

"Ireland Erin O'Brien, I've known I've loved you for the past two decades. I've let time, distance, and a freak, head injury keep us apart long enough," he said with a smile. "Will you be my wife?"

"It's the ring," I said, stunned. "How did you even know we were going to get back together?"

"I've been carrying the ring since the day I went to your house and realized you were pregnant," he admitted. "I was upset, but I still knew that we needed to be together—to be a family. I've just been waiting for the right time. And, this seemed like the right time. Please say you'll marry me. I want nothing more than to wake up every day, knowing that you and our beautiful daughter are with me."

"Yes, I'll marry you!" I screamed, as he seared my mouth with a kiss.

Epilogue

BENTLEY

I WAS PACING the length of the grooms' suite when Katie entered the room. I wasn't sure why I was so nervous as I wasn't even this nervous at the birth of my children. I was always known for being the calm and collected one—cool as the proverbial cucumber.

"How is she?" I asked.

"She's doing all right. I think she just wants to get this show on the road. It's like she's been waiting for this day her entire life," Katie said with grin.

"Sure seems that way," I said, returning her smile.

"Mom is taking good care of her in there, though. Making sure she keeps the stress at bay."

"She does tend to have that calming effect on people."

"Might I add—she looks breathtakingly gorgeous. I'm not sure if you'll be able to keep your emotions in check," she said, patting my shoulder.

"You're definitely right about that. I have a little secret," I said, going in to whisper in Katie's ear. "I've already broken down twice this morning. Don't tell anyone though. I have to keep up this tough exterior of mine, you know."

Rolling her eyes, she said, "Your secret is safe with me, James Bentley. But, newsflash, we all already know the truth about you."

"Am I that obvious?" I laughed.

"Yep! And, on that note, I should probably go check on my husband and son."

As Katie left the room, Tanner approached me from behind.

"Are you ready for this, Dad?" he questioned.

"I'm not sure you're ever actually ready for this day, Son," I said, taking a deep breath.

"One day, you'll understand. Your kids grow up in the blink of an eye. Heck, I still remember when you were just a boy playing video games, and now look at you," I laughed.

"I think I already do understand, Dad," he said, as a little curly-haired princess ran up and grabbed his leg.

"Well look who decided to join us. Aren't you just beautiful, Isabella," I said, bending over to kiss my granddaughter on the top of her head.

"She takes after her mother," Tanner said, as his wife, Mandi, came up, putting her arm around his shoulders.

"Yes, she does. Thank goodness she doesn't take after us Roberts," I said with a laugh.

"Dad, Mom told me to come get you. I guess they're ready for you in the other room," my teenage son, Grant, interrupted, pointing toward the bridal suite.

"Little brother! Don't you clean up well," Tanner said, pulling Grant into his side.

"You're just jealous that you don't look this good," Grant retorted.

"Pfft. I look WAY better dude. I mean, have you seen my wife? On second thought, don't be looking at my wife," Tanner quipped.

"You two are ridiculous. I'm not sure you'll ever grow up," I said, rolling my eyes. "Besides, we all know that I look the best of all."

"And, you wonder where they get it from?" Mandi interjected.

We were all in hysterics when the door to the suite opened

as my beautiful wife entered. It'd been over twenty years since she'd come back into my life, but she still managed to take my breath away. She looked gorgeous in her champagne-colored gown, her golden locks pulled back in an elegant updo. The only sign of her fifty-five years was a few strands of silver hair woven in amongst the blond. She worried about them so, but I'd convinced her that no one else could see them. I only knew they were there because I knew her body better than my own.

"Looks like the party has already started," she said, entering the room. "I hate to break up the fun, but Lexi's waiting for her father."

Pulling Ireland into my chest, I gave her an innocent kiss. "If she looks half as beautiful as my wife then I'm a goner," I said, kissing her once more.

"You're a goner then, Dad," she said with a faint smile. "I guarantee she'll take your breath away."

"Well, she's been doing that since the day she came into this world," I reminded her.

Wiping a few tears from her eyes, she said, "I'll give you two a few minutes before joining you."

I exited the room and walked a few feet down the hall before coming to a stop at the bridal suite. Taking a deep breath, I lightly knocked before hearing my daughter telling me to enter.

I slowly opened the door and Ireland was correct—the vision of my daughter before me took my breath away. She was absolutely stunning, every inch the belle of the ball in her white, satin gown. The strapless bodice was lined with a sheer layer of cream lace and the skirt was puffy just as I had imagined it would be.

"You look just like Cinderella, princess," I said, wrapping her in my arms.

"Thank you, Daddy," she said, twirling around me. "And, look at my shoes, we even found glass slippers. Well they aren't actually glass, but you know what I mean."

"I'm not at all surprised, Lexi. After watching Cinderella with you more times than I care to remember, I'm honestly shocked that your dress isn't blue," I said with a smirk.

"I tried, but Mom told me no," she laughed.

"Seriously, Lex. You're beautiful—both inside and out. It seems like my little girl grew up in just the blink of an eye—probably faster than I would've liked. Although I never wanted to admit it, I knew Shawn would be the one to steal you away from me. He's a good kid, Lex. I know he'll love and cherish you the way you deserve. And, if he doesn't, he'll know he has to answer to me."

"He will, Dad."

"I love you, princess," I said, giving her a gentle kiss on the forehead.

"I love you, too, Daddy. You'll always be the first man I ever loved."

There was a knock at the door before Ireland let herself in and came toward us. "Can I join you two?" she asked.

"Always," I said, pulling both my wife and daughter into my arms. "My two favorite women. I love you both so much. You, Tanner, and Grant are my entire life. I can't even begin to imagine my life without you. I remind myself every day what a lucky man I am. Trust me, I know how easy it is to lose that all in the blink of an eye."

I could tell Ireland was trying to contain her tears, "We love you too, Bentley. You're the glue that keeps our family together."

"Are you two done? I'm not using waterproof mascara, and I don't want to look like a linebacker before I begin my walk down the aisle," Lexi piped up.

"That was a mistake, Lex. If you don't think you're going to tear up the minute you see Shawn, then you're delusional. I remember the moment seeing your father on our wedding day. I instantly lost it. He's always been so handsome in a tux," she said, picking a piece of lint from my shoulder.

"Hate to break up this family trip down memory lane, but I don't think we should keep my son waiting at the altar," Katie said, barging into the room.

"Did you forget how to knock, Katheryn?" I chortled.

"Save it, Roberts. I'm just looking out for my son—being a good momma bear," she said with a mock glare.

"Can you believe our two kids are actually tying the knot?" Ireland asked.

"Actually, yes. I mean I hate to remind you, but I'm pretty sure I actually called this while they were still cooking."

"Did she just refer to Shawn and me like we're turkeys?" Lexi asked with a wide grin.

"That she did. Are you sure you really want this one to be your mother-in-law?" I asked, gesturing toward Katie. "There's still time to run. I parked the truck by the back door—just in case you changed your mind."

"I'm sure, Dad, but I love that you're always looking out for me."

"Always," I said, linking arms with my beautiful daughter—not quite ready to give her away, but knowing I didn't really have a choice.

IRELAND

I SMILED FROM the side of the room with tears in my eyes, as my husband and daughter waltzed around the dance floor to "Somewhere Over the Rainbow" during the traditional father/daughter dance. Their relationship was special—a bond between a father and a daughter that should and could never be broken. Ever since he first laid eyes on her, she'd had him wrapped around her tiny, little finger. In his eyes, Lexi could do no wrong. Even when she was skipping school, and sneaking out of the house to visit Shawn in the middle of the night—she could do no wrong.

Luckily, our daughter had grown up and had become a beautiful, successful young woman. I still thought she was rushing into marriage a bit too soon, but I knew in my heart that she belonged with Shawn. Thinking back on it, if my life hadn't thrown me the curve ball that it had, I probably would've married Bentley barely out of high school myself.

"Should we go show them up?" Grant asked, approaching me from behind.

"I'm not sure who'd be more upset, your sister or your father. They both like being the center of attention," I said, giving him a big grin. "But, you don't have to ask me twice."

"That's what I like to hear. Let's show 'em what we got, Mom," he said, linking his elbow with mine as he escorted me to the dance floor.

We swayed around the room for several minutes before Grant dipped and twirled me, just as we'd practiced in the middle of the living room all those years earlier when he'd barely reached my waist.

I saw Bentley approach Grant from behind and tap on his shoulder. "May I cut in?" he asked.

"That's up to Mom," he said, grinning at me.

"Well, I suppose I could be persuaded to dance with you, Sir," I said, as Bentley reached for my hand.

"That's good because I can be very persuasive," he said, placing his hands on my hips as we began to move as one to the rhythm of the music.

"Better not let my husband see us. He can be the rather jealous type," I whispered in his ear.

"I can't say as I blame him. Every man in this room has his eyes locked on you."

"Well the only set of eyes I care about are yours," I said, placing a gentle kiss on his lips.

We swayed across the dance floor for several minutes, both lost in each other, until a tap on my shoulder interrupted our dance.

"Aren't they just beautiful," Katie said, pointing toward Lexi and Shawn who were now showing off their skills on the dance floor. The lessons they'd taken before the wedding had really paid off. They did look so graceful out there as if they were just floating together as one.

"They are perfect," I said. "I think we all did a good job."

As if right on cue, Greg walked up carrying a silver tray with four flutes filled with only the best champagne.

"I figured we all deserved this after putting up with those two for twenty years," he chortled.

"To us," I said, taking a glass and clinking it against the others.

"And to Bentley for not killing my son," Katie added with a laugh.

"There's still time," Bentley said with a grin.

"What are you all laughing about," Lexi asked as they'd come over to join us.

"Just talking about what beautiful grandbabies you're going to give us," Katie lied.

"Mom, please don't start in on that already," Shawn pleaded.

"Shawn, have I ever told you what a smart young man you've become," Bentley said.

"Oh my god, Dad. It's my wedding day. You promised you wouldn't embarrass me," Lexi added.

"I don't recall any such agreement, Lex," Bentley shrugged.

"Just let it go, Lex. You know he won't admit it," I laughed.

"You're right. But, we came over here because he wanted to thank you both for letting us use the cabin in Tennessee for our honeymoon. We both have so many memories down there and we know you all do too."

"That we do," Bentley said, pulling me in closer to him. "So many memories have been created within those four walls. I know your grandma and grandpa would want you both to use the cabin and enjoy it."

"I wish they could be with us today. I really miss them," Lexi said, sadness in her voice.

"Me too, princess. Me too," Bentley said, pulling Lexi into our embrace. The three of us hugged and shed a few tears before letting our daughter go.

"Thank you," I said, putting my head on Bentley's chest as we continued to sway to the music.

"You're welcome, but I have no idea why you're thanking me," he admitted.

"Thank you for giving me my children, my family—a home. You reminded me that I didn't need to go through life alone— that I didn't need to constantly live in fear of loss. You never let me forget that our love has always entwined us," I said, reaching up to capture his lips with my own. "I love you, James Bentley Roberts. Never forget how much I love you."

"I could never forget you. You're a part of me, Shamrock. Even if my memory should ever again fail me—in my heart, I will always love and remember you."

Acknowledgements

FIRST AND FOREMOST, I want to thank my readers—you amaze me every single day. Without you, I wouldn't have continued on this writing journey. Your daily messages are the highlight of many of my days. The friendships I have made with many of you, I know will last a lifetime. For that I'm truly grateful. I've said it before and I'll say it again, there are so many wonderful books to choose from and I'm truly honored that you took the time to read mine. Thank you for the bottom of my heart!

To my beta readers: Kelly Williams (#JasonsLover), Katie Monson (#BusDriver), Jillian Toth, Julie Monaco (#JuicyJDavis), Susan Rayner, and Aubrea Ziegelgruber (#SisterWife)—thank you for helping me dig deeper and making Love Entwined a much more polished story. You answered my unending questions and in the process have become six of my dearest friends. Thank you and I love you all more than you will ever know!

To my Nachos: Gia Riley and Mandi Beck—thank you for keeping me grounded during this process and for really just being you. I would be lost in this world without you. You've become two of my very best friends. Thank you for your support, ideas and friendship.

To Kylie and staff at Give Me Books—thank you for helping me with the behind-the-scenes work with my cover reveal and release blitz. You have no idea how much your support means to me.

To some of the most incredible indie authors I've met during this journey. Riley Mackenzie, Tori Madison, BL Berry, Isabelle Richards, J.D. Hollyfield, Tia Louise, Stephanie Rose, Adriana Locke, RE Hunter, Kennedy Ryan, and the Indie Chicks Rock clan. Thank you for your stories, advice and friendship. There aren't enough words to express my appreciation. Love you all!

To the bloggers who have shared in the cover reveal, reviewed and promoted *Love Entwined*—none of this would be possible without your constant hard work and dedication. Your support humbles me on a daily basis—thank you!

Christina Rhoads, thank you for being you. Thank you for loving my stories and my characters more than I think I even do at times. Thank you for reminding me why I do what I do. I could go on and on, but just know you are a special person and deserve the very best out of life. I heart you, Lady!

My husband, Brian, for his support during my writing journey. For listening to me whine and giving me advice when it's needed. Thank you and I love you!

To my dad—thank you and your librarian ways for showing me at a young age that books could be pretty cool. You've always supported my ideas, some crazier than others, and I'll be forever grateful. I love you!

Please feel free to join my Facebook group, M.C. Decker's Books, to talk about Love Entwined as well as the books in the Unspoken Series.

Also, enjoy the playlist I created for Love Entwined. It can be found on Spotify.

About the Author

M.C. DECKER IS the author of the Unspoken Series and the newly released standalone novel, Love Entwined. She lives in a suburb of Flint, Michigan with her husband, Brian, and spoiled-rotten Siamese cat, Simon. For the last decade, she has worked as a journalist for several community newspapers in Michigan. She enjoys all things '80s and '90s pop culture: movies, boy bands, music and especially the color, hot pink. She also strictly lives by the motto, "Life is better in flip flops," and is a diehard Detroit Tigers fan.

Connect with M.C. Decker on

Facebook

Goodreads

Twitter

Books by M.C. Decker

Unwritten

Unscripted

The Unwritten Duet Box Set

Unwrapped

9 781534 712997